PROMISE to KEEP

USA TODAY BESTSELLING AUTHOR
J.L. BECK
NEW YORK TIMES BESTSELLING AUTHOR
MONICA CORWIN

Copyright © 2021 by Bleeding Heart Press

www.bleedingheartpress.com

Cover design by C. Hallman

Cover image taken by Wander Aguiar

Cover model: Rodiney and Dina

All rights reserved.

No part of this book may be reproduced in any form or by any electronic or mechanical means, including information storage and retrieval systems, without written permission from the author, except for the use of brief quotations in a book review.

CONTENTS

1. Valentina — 1
2. Adrian — 9
3. Valentina — 17
4. Adrian — 25
5. Valentina — 33
6. Adrian — 41
7. Valentina — 49
8. Adrian — 57
9. Valentina — 65
10. Adrian — 73
11. Valentina — 80
12. Adrian — 87
13. Valentina — 94
14. Adrian — 102
15. Valentina — 110
16. Adrian — 118
17. Valentina — 126
18. Adrian — 134
19. Valentina — 142
20. Adrian — 150
21. Valentina — 158
22. Adrian — 166
23. Valentina — 173
24. Adrian — 182
25. Valentina — 190
26. Adrian — 197
27. Valentina — 205
28. Adrian — 213
29. Valentina — 221

30. Adrian	229
31. Kai	237
About the Authors	245

1

VALENTINA

*I*t was always too good to be true.

He was too good to be true.

Hadn't life taught me that lesson over and over again, blow after blow? To be happy means a much harder fall to the bottom. And while I'm not dead yet, I'm buried in the pain of the only choice I'm left with.

But pain is an old friend. I can handle it.

I just don't know if I can handle losing *him*.

It doesn't matter, not really, when the only thing I need to think about right now is getting out of here before Adrian comes back and sees the truth stamped across my face. He reads me like a book, so there's no way I'll be able to keep this from him—not something this important. And there's no way he won't be able to punish me for it, even if it kills him too.

I race back to our bedroom, my bare feet slapping on the polished floors. Everything in our bedroom looks the same, yet now it feels different, like it's holding its breath until I'm gone.

I stop for a moment, breathing deeply, skimming my fingers over my still flat belly. It hits me. This is the same hand I used to give my father that gun. The gun that killed Adrian's mother. The realization makes me jerk my fingers away, coming full circle.

I have to run.

It only takes me a few moments to gather a few pieces of clothing, some jewelry I might be able to sell, and my phone. Nothing else. I'm careful only to take the things he gave me. I don't need any more sins staining my conscience. I don't need to give him another reason to hate me.

I grab a coat because I don't know how long I'll be outside once I'm gone and slip my feet into some practical flats Adrian would scowl at if he saw me wearing them. Not because he particularly cares about my footwear, but because he enjoys seeing me dressed up, dressed up by him.

This time, I'm silent as I tiptoe back into the hall toward the foyer. It's one quick jaunt down the stairwell, and no one will even realize I'm gone until it's too late. Kai and the crew have all been distracted since the attack, and now with the council breathing down Adrian's neck, of course, they aren't watching me closely.

No one expects me to leave.

But it's the only thing I can do to save Adrian and our baby.

I make it to the emergency staircase, and my hand is on the knob before an age-marked hand clamps over my wrist in a vise grip.

Rearing back, I jerk my hand loose, intent to run, only to find Cook standing there wearing her usual scowl on her face.

"Where do you think you're going?"

I swallow the truth and scramble for a believable lie. "Just going out for some air. I wanted to take a walk and thought I should go while it's still daylight."

When she narrows her eyes, the usual steely glint turning sharper, I know she doesn't believe a single word I just said. "Nice try, girl, but you're going to have to do better than that if you want to convince the guards at the bottom of the stairs."

Crap. I rarely go outside without Kai or Adrian with me. Those guards must peel off when they aren't needed. "How many are there?" I venture, studying her face for any clues.

She wraps her hands around her wide hips and jerks her chin at me. "Two, but all you need to do to get past them is act like the high and mighty pampered princess they expect you to be. Own the fact that you can walk out of here at any moment, and they won't question it. You might be tied up here like a princess in a castle, but to them, you're still the princess, which is a hell of a lot higher than their rank. Own it when you get to the bottom, and they won't question your ability to go freely."

I grab the handle again and pause. "Why are you helping me? You don't even like me."

Her apron shifts, pulling tight across her ample frame as she shrugs. "I don't like or dislike you. But I also don't believe in holding someone hostage if they want to leave."

I open my mouth to tell her I don't want to leave, but then I clamp it shut again and simply nod.

This time, she gently grips my hand over the door handle and turns it for me. "Get going now. You don't want to be out when it's dark."

The urge to hug her swarms me, but I tamp it down since she won't appreciate the gesture anyway.

I make it one flight of stairs before she calls after me. "Don't forget to get rid of that tracker in your arm. It's the first thing they will use to find you."

My hand slaps across the tiny scar on my forearm of its own accord, and I consider what I have to do as I run down the stairs.

I slip on the last one, almost tumbling to the cold concrete. I'm so lost in thought but manage to grab the metal railing at the last second.

"Own it," I whisper to myself, throwing my shoulders back. Then I ramp my chin up and hike my bag higher on my shoulder. I'd seen my mother do this move a million times, even when I knew she wasn't feeling anywhere near as strong as she looked.

I carefully open the door leading to the lobby and stride out like I own the place and everyone in it.

Someone says my name. "Mrs. Doubeck?"

My heart breaks all over again hearing it this way.

I spin and level the burly guard with a glare as if he interrupted my day. "Yes?"

"Um...are you? Do you need...?"

"What?" I snap, putting so much bite in my tone I shock myself.

"A car? Do you need a car?" he finishes, his shoulders slumping.

I shake my head and focus on absolutely not smiling to take some of that kicked-puppy look out of his eyes. "Thank you, but I'll manage. If anyone asks, I'll be back soon."

It takes another few seconds to clear the building, and I force myself to maintain a steady gait and not run. In a few more seconds, I realize I probably just signed that young guard's death warrant. Adrian will be hunting for me the second he returns from the council meeting, and he'll kill every one of his staff to figure out who made contact with me as I left.

I continue walking and then dig out the coat I'd brought when the chill in the air and my jangling nerves finally get to me. Right now, I only have some cash and a few pieces of jewelry. I need to make a plan and then get as far away from the city as I'm able without anyone seeing me. Easier said than done, I know.

I don't know how far I walk. Time seems to drag on when you're looking over your shoulder at every turn. All I know is that it's got to be at least a couple of hours later when I come across a seedy motel that looks like the perfect place to hide.

The girl at the front desk hands me a key in exchange for cash without even glancing up from her TV. The room looks clean enough. There aren't any bed bugs on the mattress, and the bathroom smells of bleach and lemon cleansers. *It could be much worse*, I tell myself.

I drop my bag on a worn burgundy chair and sit on the edge of the bed. The frame squeals as it takes my weight but then goes silent, leaving me to my thoughts.

First things first, I need to destroy the tracking chip Adrian put in my arm. If I leave it in, this will all have been for nothing. I stare at the tiny scar and remember how I got it. A shiver rolls through me, but I get up and head into the bathroom to see if I can find something to take care of it. There's a plastic-wrapped personal kit in one of the drawers as if someone left it behind and the cleaning staff just left it. Inside is a razor, a small first-aid kit, shampoo, soap, lotion, and if I keep digging through it, hopefully, the courage to actually do this.

I have to break open the safety razor to get the blade out. Inside the first-aid kit are a couple of Band-Aids and an alcohol swab. It's dried out, so I add a few drops of water to it and let out a long sigh of relief when the scent of alcohol hits me.

It takes me pacing the room, blade between my thumb and index finger, to get myself amped up enough. I have to do it to protect Adrian and our baby. It's the only chance we have. That thought steadies my hand as I brace my forearm on the dresser with a towel spread underneath.

My first slice is too shallow, and I don't see the tracker. Folding my lips in to stifle the pain-filled groan, I make one more cut, deeper than the first. Blood drips down my arm, but then I see the tiny nodule at the surface. I let out a shallow breath. I'm not religious, but I'm thanking whatever god is out there right now.

With slippery fingers, I carefully grasp it and pull it out. Taking it to the bathroom, I drop it on the tile floor and smash it with my foot, then flush the pieces for good measure.

After the toilet stops swirling, I notice the red splotches on the floor dripping from my arm. I race back to the towel to clean my skin, then wipe up the bathroom floor afterward.

Once the cut is cleaned up and I'm bandaged, I slip off my shoes and lie down on the bed. The practical jeans I put on earlier feel too tight. My black blouse grates against my skin as my arm throbs in time with my erratic heartbeat.

I hate this so much. For once in my life, I was happy and finally starting to believe that maybe, just maybe, someone would keep a promise to me...and I'd be safe.

The phone beside the bed rings out in a sharp blare so loud it startles me, and I scramble over the side of the bed to hide between the bed and the wall.

It continues to ring, and my mind spins. Has he found me already? Did he follow me? Did I take too long to get rid of the tracker?

What do I do? I wrap my arms around my body and hunker down, praying that when someone shows up, maybe they won't see me. I'm small and easily missed in most cases.

The phone stops ringing, and suddenly, I can hear my breathing sawing in and out of me in ragged pants. I take a few deep breaths, trying to calm myself and my heart.

The temporary safety I thought I found is fractured, broken, just like that photo of Adrian and his mother I dropped.

I grab the pillow and blanket off the bed, check all the locks on the door, unplug the cord from the phone, and then slide the closet door open to step inside.

Once I make myself a little pallet and fold myself up in the dark, I close my eyes. It's not Adrian's face that comes to mind first, but Rose's. She'd know what to do right now. Without a doubt, we'd have already crossed into Canada on our way to the nearest bar for a celebratory drink to ring in our escape.

But she's gone, and it's just me now. I have to learn how to keep myself safe. For so long, I failed...

I failed myself.

I failed Rose.

Hell, in the end, I failed Adrian too.

It led me to this moment. I'll be the mother neither of us had, and I won't fail our child. As long as I'm still breathing, I'll do whatever I have to in order to protect them. If only I could explain that to him. Maybe he'll understand and see reason? Knowing him, though, he won't stop looking for me, not for one single second until I'm back in his clutches. If only that isn't where I want to be too.

Now his face comes to mind, the soft press of his lips against my neck, right below my ear. He always knows just where to kiss me to make me shiver. Then I hear him whisper, "Angel," and it's enough to let me fall asleep.

2

ADRIAN

I don't regret killing Sal. If anyone deserved to be gutted, it was that bastard. What I do hate is being in society's crosshairs. I hate that my people are suffering because of my actions. I fucking hate that Andrea will never be the same because I failed to keep her safe.

The leather of my seat creaks while I shift, and the seat belt cuts uncomfortably across my neck until I yank it down in disgust. I spent the better part of the day listening to assholes questioning and berating me. My father would have never stood for it, yet I endured, all in hopes of ensuring Valentina's safety in the end. If I give them a reason to dig, they'll find her, and maybe, if I'm not strong enough to keep her safe too, they'll take her away.

I'll have nothing left to live for.

Michail—solid, immovable Michail—drives faster, sensing my restlessness without me having to say a word. His black curls are disheveled, making him look younger than his twenty-eight years.

He grips the steering wheel with white knuckles, and I draw in a slow and steady breath.

"If you have something to say, then say it."

He carefully shifts his hands on the wheel, sliding them around the leather to cup the circle from the bottom. His shoulders stay tight despite the casual posture, his black suit jacket bunching along the top. "I didn't like that. I don't like them watching you so closely."

His silky soft voice, threaded with steel, breaks the tension a bit. Of course, he'd be worried about me. All my men worry about me. It's the only reason I trust them so implicitly.

I settle in the seat again and reach up to grab the handlebar to stretch out my stiff shoulder. It always aches when it's about to rain, ever since my fighting days. "I don't like it either, but it won't be for long. Once they figure out there's no body, and they have no proof, there's nothing they can do to me or any of us."

"What about Andrea?" he asks.

I tighten my hold on the handle. "I will hunt those bastards down, rip their dicks from their bodies, and present them to her in a decorative box. Maybe she can have them mounted and framed. Alexei will love that."

He snorts but then sobers, remembering our friend is hurt so badly right now. "Good. All of us will help."

"But we can't do anything until this council shit is cleared up, and Valentina is safe and secure. I'll feel better when her father is dead too. Then I'll feel like no one can touch her."

The memory of her scent hits me, the silky warmth of her curls in my fingers. I'm itching to get my hands on her, ease some of this worry about her safety for a while. I don't worry when she's in my arms because no one would dare touch her. Being away from her isn't an option until everything is settled.

Which brings something to mind. I point out the window. "Turn up here and head to the second safe house. I want to check and make sure it's in order in case anyone needs to use it."

"Why not the first one?"

I scoff. "Everyone knows the first one is never really safe. It's the one all the other families seem to know about. Look at us chasing after Sal."

"We knew most of his safe houses," Michail points out.

"Yes, but that's because Kai is the best at his job. Obviously, we didn't know the most important one for far too long." Thinking about how long it took to track and kill that bastard makes me angry all over again. I tighten my grip as he makes the turn hard, scanning the rearview mirror for any tails.

The streets are already growing quiet in the post-rush-hour lull. This street in the suburbs is particularly quiet, which is why I chose it for the safe house. A quiet two-bedroom ranch in the middle of abso-fucking-lutely nowhere.

When we pull up, we scan the street for any movement—cars, people, or otherwise. The houses are far enough apart that I can't make out anyone behind curtains or in shadowed light. Perfect.

After climbing out of the car, I strip off my suit jacket and toss it into the seat before heading up the walk. It takes a minute to remember the code for the door lock, but then I walk inside. The air is stale, but everything looks clean. I flip on the lights, content the shades and curtains are drawn.

Michail surveys the empty refrigerator. "Everything is running. You want me to get it stocked, just in case?"

I nod and head into the bedroom to look things over. "Yeah, get the cleaner in here too. One we've never used before, contracted via a burner phone. I don't want a single thread leading back to us."

Coming back out, I spot Michail checking the hookups behind the big-screen TV. "What are you, checking to see if you'll be able to watch the big game here? You don't think you'll be able to see it well enough in the command center?"

He chuckles, deep and slow. A sound the women in society rarely get to hear but try for, nonetheless. "Of course not, but I can't exactly watch the game in my underwear with all of you bastards."

He stands and braces his hands on his hips, and it hits me he's going to do one of those intervention moments the guys draw straws for because they fear my reaction. "Spit it out, whatever the fuck it is," I mutter, already tired.

"If you confess, they will sentence you to death."

I draw in a long breath and hold it a moment, using it to bring the edge off my anger and my need to get Val in my arms. "You don't think I fucking know that?"

He shrugs. "Just need to remind you."

I take a step closer, and he doesn't even flinch. "Who thinks I need a reminder?"

The question is moot since we both know Kai is yet again trying to butt in where I don't need him. I turn into the kitchen and check the cabinets to give my hands something to do. "Well, you can tell him I have no intention of fucking confessing to anything."

"What if they threaten Valentina?"

I charge around the counter and have my hand on his neck before he can even think to move. He freezes in my hold, his hazel eyes going dark from my shadow. But he doesn't flinch or even breathe heavily. I lean in, my face an inch from his. "If they threaten Valentina, then it will be the end of society as we know it. I'll finally take the step my father was always too chickenshit to take and remove every single one of those bastards from power. One by one by one until they decide they don't want to lose anyone else and surrender to me."

I give him a little squeeze. "So I think it's in everyone's best interest that Valentina doesn't even get mentioned in the presence of anyone who might even go near the council or their lackeys."

Staring into my eyes, he says nothing, waiting for me to release him. By virtue of his position, he can say anything he wants to me, all my men can, but that doesn't mean there won't be consequences, as Kai learned the hard way.

My hands are shaking and cold when I slide them away from his skin. He still doesn't flinch, and I realize it's not bravado. It's trust.

Punishment is one thing, but he trusts me not to take it too far, not unless he deserves it.

Fuck. I turn away again, unable to look at him. Have I been too hard on Kai? Especially given all I've asked of him recently. When it comes to Valentina's safety, it's like I get some kind of blinders on, and my default is rage. Like the only way to make sure she stays with me is to ensure not a single person would dare come near her.

I brace my hands on the counter and roll my neck around. There won't be an apology, there never is, but I can explain myself, my thoughts, and give them a little more to go on the next time one of them needs to butt heads with me. "She is my only reason for living, Michail. Do you understand? If something happens to her, then there is nothing else left."

"Do you mean the same to her?" he asks.

I pivot to level him a glare. "Why would you ask that? Has she said something?"

He crosses his arms over his chest and shakes his head. "I just want to know that the woman I'm expected to take a bullet for, the woman you'd sacrifice everything for, would do the same for you."

I grind my teeth. "You obviously aren't hearing me. I don't want her to take a fucking bullet for me. I don't want a single scratch on her body. No one touches her. No one looks at her. No one gets even an inch too close. If they can reach her to hurt her, then you and I have already failed. Are we clear?"

If he takes even one more second to answer, I'll deck him. Finally, he nods once, his chin barely dipping. "I understand. Nothing will happen to her on my watch, I promise you."

We stay that way for a moment, measuring each other. Then I say, "Fine, let's get out of here. I want to get back to her."

I lock up the house and head toward the car. Michail follows, his soft steps barely audible on the concrete walk.

The car beeps with the unlock, and I climb in, crushing the jacket I'd forgotten I'd left there.

We pull away and head back into the city. "Stop at Velvet's place on the way. I want to get something for Valentina."

He leans over and gives me a grin. "Velvet's? Really?"

I shrug, answering his smile with one of my own. "I've never had a wife before. I want to spoil her a little bit."

He snorts, his eyes glued to the road. "A little bit? You can't get anything at Velvet's for less than a down payment on a Tesla."

Velvet's is closed at this hour, but one text from me brings the woman who owns the store running to open it for us. I survey the merchandise and pick out a necklace. Diamonds run around the length to two clusters of diamonds that look like angel wings framing a large canary-yellow diamond.

It's stunning, and my angel will look so good naked in my bed, sparkling in the overhead light with this on.

I hand it back to Velvet, and she carefully wraps it for me. "You have my account information."

Her black hair spills over her shoulder as she gives me a bow. "Of course. I hope your lady enjoys it. If not, bring her with you next time. I'd love to help you both pick something out."

I leave without another thought, the white bag inlaid with gold clutched tight in my fist. Usually, purchases at Velvet's include a security escort, but tonight, it's just Michail.

We climb back into the car, and I settle into the seat again. This time, my jacket is in the back as Michail moved it for me when I exited at Velvet's.

"Home?"

I nod and face out the window, my mind already on Valentina. "Home," I whisper.

It takes way too long to get there, and I'm itching as I exit the elevator. My heart hits my feet when she's not standing there waiting.

Maybe she's fallen asleep early. I head up to the bedroom, but it's also empty.

Hearing Kai's footsteps behind me make me stiffen, and he says what I could already feel if I had stopped to focus.

"Valentina is gone."

3
VALENTINA

Rose and I would have never made it. It's not just the cheap motel—well, that's part of it—but compounded with the scratchy sheets, the constant racket from the other rooms, and the strange odor that comes out of the sink drain every time I brush my teeth...yeah, we wouldn't have made it on our own.

As I sit on the bed with the springs digging into my ass, I think about all of the abuse we suffered through, and I'm reminded that I'm spoiled. Even more so under Adrian's care since I don't fear bruises on a daily basis with him, at least not any I won't remember fondly. We'd have fled the house and been back within a week, or at least, I might have.

Under threat of death for both my child and me, here I am, whining to myself over the crappy motel room and how badly I slept last night. I'm spoiled, and I'm selfish.

I swipe roughly at the tears that seem to constantly fall now and lever off the bed to grab my shoes. The small diner in the parking lot will likely give me food poisoning, but I don't have anything else to eat. I've been researching pregnancy on my phone, and it tells me I need to eat lots of lean proteins and iron to help the baby grow healthy. Somehow, I also need to hunt down a phone charger since I forgot one in my haste to rush out the door. Maybe someone at the diner will let me borrow theirs.

It's a short walk, but even so, I feel exposed outside the hotel room. My black pants and silk blouse don't exactly fit in here, and I'm terrified he has people out hunting for me. I'd shoved my hair into a worn baseball cap I'd found in the closet, so I'll likely have lice to deal with after the food poisoning.

I scramble into a booth, and a little old lady in a smeared apron pours a glass of water and waits with an expectant brow for me to order.

Trying to keep things simple, I order eggs and toast. Hopefully, I'll be able to keep them down and save me from having to make another trip here for dinner later. The woman, her name tag reads Sammy, heads back into the kitchen, and I hunch down in the booth with my arms wrapped around my middle. It's painfully obvious I need a plan, and hiding out in a motel room isn't going to cut it. I've little doubt Adrian will send people after me. If I want to stay alive and keep my baby alive, I need to get out of the city.

The thought of leaving, of him never finding me, rips open some of the realities I haven't let myself face yet. How can I take care of a baby on my own with barely any money and no job? Once he's born, how can I look at him every single day and see Adrian in his eyes and not want to go back to him and beg for forgiveness?

The thought of never seeing him again makes me ill, even more so than the tiny person growing inside me. I rub my hand over my belly. It's still flat, of course, but I can imagine it growing and how I'll feel the closer I get to him being born.

Sammy returns quickly with eggs and toast that don't look half bad, or maybe I'm too hungry to really care.

After I shovel it down and pay, I head back to the motel room and survey what I've got to work with. Not much, really. Some clothes, a cell phone, a few pieces of jewelry, and a small wad of cash I found in the bag I'd gathered everything up in.

Nothing of great value and nothing that will tell me how to get myself out of this mess to safety. That's all I really want…something I miss more than anything. In Adrian's arms, I felt safe. Like nothing in the world could reach me. Now, all I feel is adrift. My insides feel hollowed out like a melon in summer.

The phone vibrates, the cook calling, and I quickly answer. "Hello."

"Still alive, I see."

I snort. "Well, if the lice don't get me, the food might, so…your day might look up in the end." I smile at myself. It's the kind of answer Rose would have given. She was always the strong one. An ache to hold her hand again clenches around my heart. It's not the same as the pain I feel missing Adrian, though. They both scar my insides in different ways.

"I'm going to meet you tonight and bring you a care package. Something to help you survive until the heat dies down, so you can get out of town." The fact she's telling me my plan word for word seems like maybe it's a tad too predictable. Probably not good.

After another minute of rambling about security at the penthouse, she hangs up, and I clutch the phone to my chest. How did she become my only lifeline right now? Even though she helped me escape and is helping me with supplies, I don't trust her. I don't know how I'll trust anyone for the rest of my life. The thought makes me sad.

I wipe away a new round of tears and lie back on the bed. Suddenly, I'm so exhausted I can't keep my eyes open.

I wake to a heavy pounding on the door. At first, fear claws at me. Oh, God, he's found me already.

But then the cook's surly voice calls through the door. "It's cold, and I don't want to stand out here all night."

I throw the covers off and race to unlock the chain. The second the door is open, she sweeps inside and peers out the ratty curtains. "I don't think anyone followed me. They all thought I didn't like you anyway, so…they have no reason to think I'd help you escape."

I reach out to hug her in thanks, but she holds me off. "I still don't like you, girl, so back off."

"Sorry," I mumble and sit on the edge of the bed. "Thank you for coming."

She unwinds a gray scarf from her neck and tosses a heavy bundle on the bed beside me. "That's a few things I took from the kitchen no one will miss, and then a couple of other things I thought you might need."

I untie the top of the bag and peer inside. Some food I can eat without much fuss, a charging cable (how did she know?), and a heavy black—

"You brought me a gun. Whose is it?"

"No one will miss it. I didn't take it from the armory at the penthouse, so don't worry. I'm not an idiot."

I scowl at it in the bag and then close the top of it, so I don't have to see it anymore right now. Guns still make my skin crawl.

"Any news, are they all looking for me?"

She nods. "Everyone is out hunting for you right now. All the men who can look are doing so, and your man is stalking back and forth like a caged beast at the penthouse in case you come back there, or someone contacts him about a ransom."

Guilt bites hard, and I lean over to stifle the pang in my middle. "I hate this. I so hate this. I keep thinking if I go back—"

"He'll kill you," she deadpans. "He'll drag you in the door and murder you right there in the entryway. He doesn't tolerate any weakness, and you've made him vulnerable in a way he's never been. Hell, he wouldn't be under watch by the council if it weren't for you."

She's right. Of course, she's right. I have to stay away. In more than just keeping his son safe, I'll be helping him, protecting him. "Okay. I'll try to keep moving and head out of town. Maybe in the early morning hours, I can make it to a new motel and just keep jumping until I can catch a ride out for good."

She nods, her lined face set grimly. "That's a good start. Just keep moving and use what I gave you there if you feel like you're in danger. Just be careful, all right?"

I nod, wanting to tell her I'm not a complete idiot, but I doubt she'll trust my judgment there. "Thank you for helping me, by the way. If there's anything I can do for you when I get out of here, please let me know."

"I don't want anything from you, girl. I just didn't want you to throw your life away. Watch him kill you one way or another until you're gone for good."

It's almost the nicest thing she's ever said to me, but I don't call her out on it since she won't take it kindly. I simply nod.

She throws her scarf back around her neck and marches toward the door. "Remember what I said, be careful. I'll check in with you again tomorrow and see where you are and if there is anything I can do to help, but I might have to stay away for a couple of days, so no one suspects anything."

I open the door for her. "Thanks again."

She leaves without another word, and I lock all the locks behind her. I'm tired but still scared. For some reason, I climb back into the closet with the blanket and huddle up on the floor. It's about the same comfort level as the bed. The bag is still sitting on the bed, and I don't have the heart to look inside again. She'd given me a gun as if I could possibly use it. Hell, I couldn't even use it when I should have to protect Rose and me.

I rub my belly again and whisper softly to the baby inside. It'll be a long time until he hears me, but for now, it comforts me in a strange way. I'm doing this for him, and it's something I can't afford to forget.

The neighbors start screaming at each other, and I can hear them through the wall. The yelling shifts to a physical altercation, and suddenly, I'm back in that house under my dad and Sal's fists. No, I won't go back to that. Sal is dead, and I never have to go back to that.

In a full circle, my gut clenches again as guilt pounds into me. Adrian took care of me. He saved me, and this is how I repay him...by running off when he's facing down our enemies?

I surge out of the closet, grab the corner of the bag, and drag it to me. Then I reach inside and wrap my fist around the pistol grip of the gun. It takes a second to remember how to check the chamber, the safety, and the bullets, but it comes back quickly. As does the nausea of holding the cold metal tight in my hands. It bites into my palm, but I settle into my nest again, setting it on the floor, my fingers still gripping it.

If he's coming after me, I need to be ready to protect myself. Kai is likely the threat I'll face, and I'm prepared to force him not to turn me in based on his oath. I don't know if it will stand, him being so loyal to Adrian and all...but I have to try.

I look down at the gun. My only other option is to shoot him, and I really don't want to kill Adrian's best friend on top of running away. This isn't meant to be a punishment for him. I'm just trying to keep our baby safe, myself safe, and keep Adrian from damning his soul completely.

If he comes after me and somehow kills us, he'll never forgive himself. If I go back and he kills us, he'll also never forgive himself.

So my only choice is not to get caught.

4
ADRIAN

*I*f one more person asks me if Valentina walked out on her own, I'm going to start shooting them in the face. Let them line up to put my Magnum in their mouth, and maybe they will stop asking me stupid fucking questions.

I pace the foyer of the penthouse, not wanting to leave for fear she'll need me when I get her back. My men are scouring every inch of the city, and I have Kai's spies working overtime to feel out the society and the council for any whiff of her. So far, they've turned up nothing.

She's the goddamn daughter of one of the ranking members, the wife of another, and no one has spotted her? Whether it's willful ignorance to get under my skin or someone is hiding her very well, I can't wait to rip the balls off the bastard who thought he could take from me.

If Sal's greasy ass were still alive, I'd be so far in his business he wouldn't be able to think straight. As it stands, I have my guys digging even further in his family to see if they can turn over any answers. I wouldn't put it past them to take her in retaliation for Sal's death. Not that they have a body to prove anything.

I keep pacing and watching the elevator. Every time it moves, I feel like my heart is going to pop out of my mouth. I'm riding on caffeine and sheer adrenaline at this point since I can't sleep without her beside me in our bed. I can't rest knowing she is out there and could be hurt, or scared, or dying.

When my nerves are frayed, and I can't take the silence anymore, I call together my five. At least the ones who can go into the field right now. Kai, Ivan, Michail, and Alexei. While I'd usually excuse Alexei to stay by his injured twin's side, I can't spare him until I know my angel is on her way back to me.

I pace the command room in circles around them, like a shark circling for the kill. "It's been twenty-four hours. Why don't we have answers? What about the tracker?"

Kai, as usual, speaks first. Even now, amid this crisis, his suit is pressed, and his dark hair is perfect. Hell, even his tanned skin is glowing in the command room's lights. "We have round-the-clock patrols trying to hunt her down. Our contacts at the police are involved, searching for her too. Everyone is doing everything they can. And the tracker was disabled somehow."

What he's not saying rings loudly in the room. Echoing so loudly, I expect someone to repeat the words they are all thinking out loud. "Bring up the footage again," I order, not giving them a chance to voice what I know they're thinking.

Michail is closest to the controls and cues up the footage we've all watched at least a dozen times by now. In the images, she's the same as ever. As I look at her on the screen, my chest collapses in on itself. My fingers ache with the need to touch her, claim her, bring her back into my arms and never release her again.

As if anticipating my next order, Michail loads all the footage we have of her leaving on a loop. It's the same no matter how many times I watch it. She walks out, bag in hand, so confident that when I first saw it, I expected she might return. I'd punish her, but then we'd move on. But now, it's been too long to expect her to come back—not of her own volition. And if she knew the punishments I've been thinking about, she'd never return.

Of course, that is if she left on her own. The footage seems to lead to that conclusion, but I can't rectify the woman who laid in my arms just last night with the woman who walked away from me, from us, so easily. Either someone got to her, which is impossible since access to my penthouse is strictly contained, or she really left.

The thought circles my brain over and over like the looped footage. *She left me. She left me. She left me.*

"No!" I shout.

Every eye shifts toward me, away from the screen. No one has the balls to call me on how far down the rabbit hole I'm going with her gone. The memory of her is the only thing holding me to my sanity right now, and the thought of punishing whoever took her is my only reason for living.

I'm tired of the way they're all looking at me, so I head out of the command room toward our bedroom, hoping to find a clue. She took some of her belongings with her...some clothes and some jewelry, I think. I've bought her so much over the past few months, I can't be sure.

If she took the jewelry, she needs money. But why? We have money, and she knows I will stop at nothing to make her happy. So why would she pack a bag, take her clothing and jewelry, and walk out?

What could have caused her to go if not someone saying something or doing something to make her think it's her only choice?

I stalk through the bedroom on a loop, keeping my eyes off the bed for fear of destroying it in my rage.

There is no reason for her to leave me. Not unless she found out about…

No. She couldn't have because the only person who knows about the night I rescued her is Kai. And Kai would never betray me.

But doubt creeps in easily along the tendrils of rage, of anger, of her possible betrayal. The only thing I asked of her was to never leave me. Never walk away from me like my mother did all those years ago.

If she loved me, then she wouldn't have done this. No.

I swing back around to someone having taken her. She was obviously lured out of the building under a threat of some kind.

I return to the command room; everyone has left except Kai, who is once again studying all the footage we have of her. In the shots, she calmly walks down the staircase, then out through the lobby. She speaks to the guards and then leaves the building. The street cameras show her going east, but then we lose her around a corner. Since that moment, I don't have any sight of her and no reports of anyone having seen her.

Kai stops the recordings and sits back in the chair, hands folded over his stomach. "You know what I'm thinking, what we are all thinking, Boss. You have to be thinking it too."

He's right, but I won't put it into words, not until I find her and hear the truth from her own mouth. "You all may be thinking it, but you'll keep your fucking lips shut, or I'll make them stay that way permanently."

After my threat, he goes quiet, no doubt worried I've lost my shit. Maybe I have. Maybe my angel is the only thing that has been keeping me tethered to my sanity all this time.

"What do you want to do next?" Kai asks.

I stop pacing and glare at him. "Are the guards from the lobby being questioned?"

His jaw goes tight, but he nods once, clipped. "Yes, Ivan has them. Although, I do think they are innocent."

If Ivan has them, they won't walk out of the room alive again. Innocent or guilty, they let Valentina walk out of the building, and for that, they deserve Ivan's special attention.

"The men turning against us won't help in the search," he says after a lingering silence.

Something inside me fractures, splinters, and I launch myself at him. He doesn't fight back as I topple us both to the floor. I hit him once, hard on the jaw, and the pain sings through me, tightening the bolts, battening the hatches. Yes. This is what I need.

I punch him again and again, but he doesn't fight back. His body is limp as I grasp the front of his suit, holding him in place. "Fight back, you asshole," I order.

He meets my eyes and shakes his head. "No, I deserve it. I was here when she left too. You haven't punished me yet. Apparently, I didn't learn my lesson from the last time."

The last time someone snuck past him and almost took her from me. This time, she really is gone, and the pain I felt at the mere idea of her loss before is nothing compared to this hollow ache inside me now. With her gone, there's nothing good in the world and absolutely no reason not to crush every single soul under my heel until they do my bidding.

Kai exhales loudly through his mouth, his bleeding nose not allowing him to breathe properly. I shove him to the ground and step over his body. At the bar in the corner, I grab the ice bucket and thrust my fist inside.

The chill takes some of the ache out of my knuckles, and I turn to face Kai again. He's dragged himself off the floor and reset his nose. I throw some ice cubes in a rag and hand them to him. Without a word, he presses the cold compress to his face.

This is not the man I'm supposed to be. I'm not my father, who used violence to calm himself. Sure, I like pain, but not to deliver it. Not unless it's righteous justice. And Kai would cut off a limb before he betrayed me.

I throw myself in one of the chairs and study the frozen picture of her leaving on the screen. "I need her back," I whisper.

Then I look at him, my second-in-command, and let him see the sheen of tears in my eyes. "Without her, the world will burn, and me along with it. I won't live without her. Even if she did walk away from me, I'll lock her in our bedroom after dragging her back, kicking and screaming, and that will be our lives. She promised me everything the day we got married, and I intend to make sure she makes good on that vow."

Kai rights the chair we threw over and sits beside me. "We'll find her. I promise, no matter what, we'll find her."

In my mind, no matter what means dead or alive. Which is another outcome I haven't allowed myself to consider. What if she's already dead, and that's the reason there hasn't been any sign of her?

The list of people who would love to see her bleeding out is short. Sal's family comes to mind immediately, and maybe her father. Would he rather see his little girl dead than married to me?

Probably, but if he's taken her from me, I'll make what I did to Sal look like a fucking picnic before I finish with him. Either way, her father's blood will be on my hands one day. It's just a matter of sooner or later.

"Has her father made any moves?" I ask.

My knuckles are swollen and purple, but nothing is broken. I swivel the chair to get a look at Kai's face. Nothing more than bruises now that he's set the break.

Kai doesn't say a thing about the beating I gave him. I don't know if I'm ashamed or grateful. "Not that my men have told me. I'll check in with them again. What now, Boss? Tell me what you need, and I'll take care of it."

I shove out of the chair and head toward the door. Only one thing will ease this void inside me. "I need her found, Kai. Now. Before I do something I can't apologize for later."

5
VALENTINA

The next day, I plan to check out of the motel and head to another one. At the very least, to try to cover my tracks. It's midmorning, later than I want to leave, but I've been too afraid to walk out the door for fear of someone seeing me and reporting back to Adrian.

A knock on the door makes me freeze mid-motion while packing up my bag. I ignore the sharp knock and pray they go away. Maybe it's housekeeping. Not that I've seen much of that since checking into this dump.

I gently shove the extra shirt I'm holding into the bag, straining to listen at the door. Another sharp knock makes me jump. This time, though, I drop my belongings, grab the gun, and shove it into the back of my pants. It's dangerous, but it's not like she'd given me a holster along with the weapon.

My phone vibrates, and I snatch it up. It's from Cook, who tells me to open the door.

I breathe out in relief, my shoulders relaxing. Thank goodness. I feared I might actually have to shoot someone there for a second. And I still don't know if I have the balls to do it.

Was that what I found so attractive about Adrian? He's never afraid to do the hard things...especially when it comes to keeping me safe.

I unlock the door, working my way from the chain down to the deadbolt, and open it. But Cook's not standing on the other side. It's my father.

His hair is whiter and shorter, slicked back away from his face. It also looks like he's lost some weight. Overall, he just seems old. Older than I remember when we went to the season-opening ball all those months ago.

"What are you doing here?" I stammer, still shocked at his presence.

He shoves me aside to enter my room, scowling at the surroundings. "Hopefully not catching hepatitis," he sneers, then turns to me. "Shut the door, or anyone might see us talking and come after you, dear."

The nickname isn't a sweet epithet. It's his way of mocking me. Of calling attention to the fact that biologically I'm his daughter, but I'm all but useless to him. I close the door if only to give me a moment to think. The last time we were in the same room together, he was about to leave for a business trip to New York. He left me with Sal all that time, knowing what kind of man he was and what he might do without my father's supervision.

I lock the door and face him, keeping my back against the cold metal of the exit just in case I need to make a break for it. "I'll ask you again, what are you doing here?"

He takes a quick walk around my room, which is all anyone needs since it's not very big. Then he sits on the bed, testing the squeaky springs. "Charming? How can you live in this hovel?"

"It's none of your concern. Why are you here? How did you find me?"

Once upon a time, I might have been too chickenshit to talk to him this way. To speak to him like he's in the wrong when he so often is. Even as he belittles me, he looks so old, so fragile. While studying him, I realize I no longer care what he thinks of me. I couldn't care less, in fact. It's an almost dizzying realization.

I've hated him for years because of what I endured from both his hand and then Sal's. How could he let that happen to his own child? It's so clear to me now, he let it happen because he doesn't see me as his child at all. In his eyes, not one single part of me is his blood. That's how he rationalizes my treatment. And he never bothered with Rose because she really wasn't his blood.

I stare him down, letting him see my loathing, my hate of him, in my eyes. The obedient daughter who only wanted his approval is gone. She died that night, tied to her own bed. This woman is Adrian's wife. This woman is a Doubeck, and Doubecks cower to no one. "You can leave now, Father. I'll spare you the indignity of being thrown out if you leave soon."

"So, you're pregnant with that bastard's child, aren't you? Did you run because you feared he'd kill you like he did his own pop? I wouldn't put it past him. He'll stand for nothing challenging his position of power, especially a woman."

I know I shouldn't rise to his bait, but I can't help it. "You don't know anything about him or our relationship. So don't sit there thinking you know me and why I decided to leave him."

He growls low and angry in his old senile way of his. "Girl, don't speak to me that way, or I'll make you regret it."

I narrow my eyes and stare him down. "You had to sit on the bed since you can't stand for very long without shaking...I seriously doubt you have the strength to inflict much damage on me. Save your threats for someone who might actually believe you. I'll speak to you however I want since you came here to my motel room to mock me. Now leave before I force you out of here."

He settles back on the bed like I've issued him a challenge. "I'll cut that baby from your womb before I see him have an heir. You don't understand what you're bringing into this world. His family line needs to die with him."

I lean in, unable to help it, not when he's being such an asshole. "Just like yours will, old man. I took his name, and so will his son. You have nothing and no one left to carry on your legacy. I hope you die alone and afraid. It'll be what you deserve."

"I do know one thing," he spits at me. "You have no protection. What do you think will happen when the rest of society finds out you're running around out here in the world, carrying his baby with no protection? They will be lining up to see it ripped from you before you even start to show."

The thought hasn't occurred to me that anyone would find out, but this bastard will make sure everyone knows unless I give him what he wants. I skirt the bed and pace at the end, not caring if he has to crane his neck to look at me now. After a moment, I round on him. "What the hell do you want? You haven't taken enough from me, so you have to take my child, my life from me too?"

"It's what you deserve," he says, his tone so full of venom it stings going down even though I don't care about what he thinks. He advances, moving closer to me. "Your mother died, and you didn't. In my mind, all these years, I was getting justice for her death."

I rear back, staring at him, my mouth hanging open. "I was a child. You're blaming me for my mother's death when I was a child. How could I have saved her when I barely survived myself? No thanks to you on either account."

His hand snaps out and strikes me right across the cheek.

It stings, but it's nothing compared to everything I've dealt with from Sal. I barely flinch and continue to look into his old milky eyes. "Does that make you feel manly? Hitting me? Because I have to tell you, Dad, you're losing your strength. Now, get the hell out of here. I'll only say this one more time. Leave now, or I'll throw you out myself."

When he stands, I think he's finally come to his senses and is going to go. Which will leave me the task of figuring out how he found me in the first place before I disappear for good.

But he doesn't simply stand. He shifts his weight and launches a punch right at my gut. I twist at the last second, his fist hitting my hip bone hard enough to make my skeleton rattle. I retreat, intent on putting distance between us, but he doesn't let me.

Taking hold of my shoulder, he squeezes hard and rears back for another strike. This time, I block the hit, but it still hurts. I try to wiggle from his grip, but his fingers are strong, and he's holding tight.

Instead, I move so he can't get a clear strike and has to try harder to keep me in his grip. It takes another moment for me to finally dislodge him and put the bed between us. I'm crying even though I'm more angry or sad than in pain.

"Pathetic," he sneers.

I swipe at my face with the back of my hand and prepare for his next attack. This time, I won't let him get a hold of me. He has no idea what I've already sacrificed to keep my baby safe. Getting rid of him is nothing compared to ripping my own heart out and leaving it behind.

"Get out!" I scream at him. "Go now, or the cops will show up, and you'll have to deal with them."

He snorts. "And when they show up, they will deliver you right back to your degenerate husband. So you can deal with me, or you can deal with him. And trust me, he isn't the forgiving type."

While I fear Adrian's wrath, I refuse to allow my father to win. Not like this, and not when I'm free of my feelings for him for the first time in my life. Free of his toxicity and free of having to look at his ugly face again.

I hop up on the bed to get to the door, but he intercepts me there. "We aren't through here. If you don't let me take care of it, I'll drag you home and have someone take a coat hanger to you. Then I'll make sure you'll never be able to get pregnant again. Your choice."

I rear back and spit in his face. "Fuck you."

He sneers and wipes his wrist down his face. "Oh good, you want to fight. The coat hanger it is, and I'll be sure to tell them you don't tolerate pain medication well. It'll teach you the lesson you deserve, girl."

We struggle, but somehow, he's stronger than me, tugging me toward the door and fiddling with all the locks. While he's distracted, I try to yank my arm free, but his grip is like iron, and I can't shake him off me.

I keep fighting until he curses and digs into his pocket to reveal a stun gun.

No. If he knocks me out, he can do anything he wants to me while I'm unconscious.

It's like my brain goes blank. One minute, the fear is taking hold, threatening to dislodge sanity in place of horror. Next, the world is silent, still, like a slow-motion clip in a movie.

I reach behind my back with my free arm and wrap my hand around the grip of the gun. Then I tug it out of my pants, flipping the safety off at the same time.

He pulls me tight against him, raising the Taser toward my belly. He's going to stun me right at uterus level, and I don't know if my baby can survive that.

I raise the gun and shove it into his ribs, not even bothering to aim, and pull the trigger.

The sound rips through the room, making my ears ring. His eyes go wide, and then I feel the wet hot flow of blood over my hands, wrists, down the front of me as he releases me.

He hits the floor with a thud, and I stare down at him. Red stains my fingers and his shirt front, and it's leaking into the carpet.

So much blood. It's everywhere.

I think about Rose's face in the dark and stare down at my dying father until he takes his last breath.

6

ADRIAN

Drinking sounds good. I don't do it often because I hate how it makes me feel out of control, but without her...I already feel like my soul has been ripped from my body. I won't control anything ever again.

I sip the bourbon and lay my head back against the chair. Even only two drinks in, I'm thankful my men don't see me like this. I'm ashamed of myself. Ashamed of being proved the fool at her hand. Of being used like a puppet by someone I thought truly cared for me.

What I can't get past is what I saw in her eyes. She loved me...was I too rough with her after I killed Sal? Is my barbarism why she felt the need to run? Shame, hot, sticky like maple syrup erupts inside my stomach. If I scared her away, this is what I deserve.

I take another drink and let it burn its way down to my gut. Right now, it's the only thing I'm letting myself feel. Everything else is too much.

My phone vibrates on the nightstand, but I ignore it until it goes silent again. The bottle of liquor sits by my feet, and I bend over, the room reeling, to pour another glass. Even as the liquid sloshes over the sides, I want more. If I could drown myself in it, I would. At least right now, at this moment.

The phone rings again, the buzzing vibrations breaking through my alcohol haze to the anger barely banked beneath. No one important would be trying to contact me right now. Not after I've lost her.

I stare at the device, glass raised to my lips, and it rings again, vibrating several times, then stopping. Who the fuck is calling me? I try to reason, but the liquor is doing its job of dulling my senses and turning logical thought into mush.

In the quiet again, I drink deeply and hug the crystal glass to my chest. Yes, this is what I need. An escape. Something to dull the pain enough to keep going. A tiny part of my brain says I can use this anger, this hurt, this shame, and this fear to strike out at my enemies. Finally take them down once and for all. With nothing to lose, no one would be stupid enough to stand against me. Valentina is a liability. She always has been.

It doesn't make this knife in the gut any easier to take.

The phone vibrates again, and the molten core over my anger cracks and shatters. I throw the glass against the wall above the bed, seize the phone, and scream into the receiver.

"What the fuck do you want?"

On the other end of the line is soft, ragged breathing. I strain to hear it over my own pounding heartbeat blasting in my ears. "Who is this?" I snarl.

Then a tiny shaking voice whispers, "Valentina. But it's not…it's I…don't please…"

Her words run together in a rush, barely audible.

I clutch the phone in both hands and sink to the floor in a puddle of bourbon and glass. It cuts through my pants, soaking and mixing with blood. "Val? Angel, is that you?"

I don't feel pain. All that matters in this instant is her.

"Yes. Angel. Yes."

She sounds strange, ragged, and scared. "Tell me where you are. Tell me, and I'll come get you. You sound like you need help. Let me help you."

The haze of the liquor is still present, but I can see and feel around it now. She's within my grasp, and I only have to reach out and coax her back into my arms. Then I'll never fucking let her go again. "Tell me, Angel. Tell me where you are? Let me get you home safely."

"Safe. No. Safe," she whispers as if her mouth is pressed directly into the speaker of a phone. It's not one I know of because I've had her phone traced. She must have gotten a new one or is using the one where she's been staying since she left.

I hit the mute button on the phone and scream for Kai, who has been lingering around my door like he fears I might do something stupid. "Kai! Get your ass in here now."

He comes running in, his dress shirt untucked, no tie, and barefoot. "What is it, Boss?"

In a second, he takes in the alcohol and the blood and rushes to my side, even as his own feet get cut on the glass. "Let's get you—"

I shake him off. "Get the fuck off me. It's Valentina on the phone, calling my phone. Go trace the fucking location!"

He rushes out without another word, and I unmute and continue to listen. She's panting and mumbling into the receiver, and I'm trying to pick apart every word, but I'm getting nothing.

"Val, baby, please...tell me where you are? Please." I'll beg...I'll do anything to get her back.

She mumbles louder, and I catch the word father and hiding, but everything else is muffled, not helped by whatever phone she's using. It must be cheap, or service is shit where she's located. "Come on, baby. You're stronger than this. I know you can tell me where you are. Let me help you."

I cradle the phone against my shoulder and strip my clothes off on the way to the closet. In seconds, I've changed into new pants and a clean shirt. The blood on my shins and feet will hold for now. Nothing major was injured. The room will smell like very expensive bourbon for some time, though.

"Talk to me, Val," I order as I button my cuffs and then tuck my shirt into my slacks. "Come on, baby. Give me something."

Once I get my feet jammed into shoes, despite the pain, I race out of the room and down the hall to Kai and Michail, who are on babysitting duty tonight. As if one of them could stop me from doing anything.

I stare up at the monitors while Kai types on the computer in a frantic rhythm. "Come on, you bastard. Go faster. We need to get to her. Something is wrong. I can feel it, and I can hear it in her voice."

He ignores me and continues his work as Michail shoves some weapons in his holsters and studies the map from the gun vault in the corner. "Any ideas?" he asks a moment later as the pinpoint on the city map still roves.

"Val, help me out here. Tell us where to find you. We'll come help."

She mumbles and sobs, then lowers her voice even more to a whisper. "He's going to hurt me for this, so bad. He'll make me regret it."

Fear spikes through me, sharp and biting, cutting the haze of the liquor even more. Is she talking about me? I hate the fear in her voice.

It tears me in half. I'm stuck between hunting her down to make her pay for leaving me and enfolding her in my arms to keep her safe from everything…including myself.

I swallow down a wave of bile. Dammit. When we were together, I got rough, but I thought we were on the same page, that she understood and could take it. She said she could do that for me. Did she lie?

The computer beeps, and I slap Kai on the shoulder as the dot stops in one of the shittiest neighborhoods right in her father's territory. I race out the door with Kai and Michail on my heels. "Hang on, Angel, I'm coming. Stay there. Don't you dare fucking leave, or I will hunt your ass down and make you regret it."

It feels like it takes years to load into the SUV and head across town to the seedy motel on the map. Why is she hiding there? It's near the edge of the city, so maybe she planned to stop there until she could get farther out of town. If she'd succeeded, I might not have ever found her. The thought makes me cold, frost-ridden, and uneasy. No. We'll get her back, and I'll make sure she never runs away again.

I hold the phone harder to my ear. "Still there, Angel? We're coming. Don't worry, it'll all be fine."

Another mumble, and then the line goes dead. I curse and hurl my phone at the dashboard. "Drive, Kai. Drive like your life depends on it because if I miss her, I will shoot you in the head and then shove you out the door to chase her down."

As usual, he doesn't respond to my threats but does follow my order. "We'll get her, Boss. She can't get out of that neighborhood before we get there, and those people...they are poor and will help find her if she's already made a run for it. We'll get her."

I'm terrified he's wrong, and I'm terrified he's right. When I get her back in my arms, I don't know what I'll do. My emotions are hot and cold, and I'm torn between shoving her down to claim her and slitting her throat for making me feel this way and then running. I can't stand it, and I can't live without it.

We pull up to the motel, and there's only one room with a light on. I'm out of the car before Kai's even pulled to a stop. The door is locked, and I ram into it, determined to get it open. When the lock chain finally snaps, I freeze, taking in the tableau beyond the doorframe.

Valentina is standing over her father's body, blood pooling around him on the floor. Her shirt and jeans are covered in it. Her hand, gripping a black pistol, is coated as well.

She jerks her eyes to mine as we slowly enter, and she raises the gun and backs into the closet. "No, no. No. No. No. No. Don't come any closer! Stop."

I hold my hands up in surrender as I take small steps toward her. Kai is behind me, Michail on his tail, both men mimicking my pose. One goes left and the other right.

Her hands are shaking as she aims the weapon. I keep my eyes locked with hers. "Look at me, Angel. Calm down. It's okay. You're safe now."

"I had to do it." Her voice shakes as she explains. "I couldn't let him hurt me again. Not again."

I glance at the body as my feet hit the puddle of blood. There's a Taser in his hand, clutched tight in his dead hands. I really can't say I'm sad he's gone, nor that Valentina got to be the one to take his miserable life. Except she doesn't look so good.

Shock. It has to be shock.

"Calm down. It's okay. You're safe. Put the gun down, and we can get out of here. He can't hurt you again, I promise."

She blinks and looks down at her father. Then the gun slips from her hand to hit the floor, the sound buffered by the cheap ratty carpet. How did she find this hellhole?

Kai reaches down and snatches the gun from her reach. "No serial number. That'll make things easier."

I charge forward now and grab her hard, wrapping my arms around her entirely. She doesn't resist, only stands there letting me hold her, rigid and breathing in ragged pants.

"Angel," I whisper into her hair. She's wearing an old baseball cap that smells stale and moldy, so I toss it away. Underneath, her pinned-up curls smell the same...they smell like her, and I breathe her in. "Angel, I've got you. Let's get out of here so Kai can handle this mess. Don't worry, nothing will happen to you. Your father got what he deserved."

I pull away only enough to look down at her face. She looks pale, and tears still pour down her cheeks. Suddenly, she clamps her hands on my arms, frantic and crazed. "I had to do it. I had to protect him. You believe me, don't you? You believe me?"

7
VALENTINA

I've never thought of myself as particularly strong. Not like Rose was. Right now, the idea of being strong is mocking me. Every part of my body is trembling, and all I can do is cling to Adrian while he drags me stumbling toward the car parked outside the motel room. I don't see any of the other faces as I pass them by, and I don't hear anything but my heartbeat in my own ears. That, and the sound of the gunshot on repeat in my mind. The hot sticky wetness of my father's blood clinging to my fingers, to my clothes.

I'm seconds from breaking. Something inside me finally snaps under the pressure. My father tried to ruin me for years, and it's almost ironic he'd succeed but only by forcing me to take his life. Sal is gone. My father is gone. Rose is gone. I'm the only one left.

I clutch my hand over my stomach and tuck my chin, hoping he doesn't read me, like he always does, so easily.

Even though he's probably going to kill me, the grip of his hand is offering me the tiniest bit of comfort, the only thing keeping me clinging to sanity at this point.

The world goes fuzzy, and I hear the gunshot again, so loud, echoing in my head.

I'm bodily picked up and set on the warm leather of the SUV. Adrian is gone, the door closed in my face, but then he's come around to slide in beside me behind the driver's seat.

"Angel," he whispers.

A hot tear slides down my cheek. Why is it hot? Oh, I'm freezing. That's why I'm shaking. I feel so cold I expect to see my breath fogging out in front of me with every exhale. But no, it's inside me. What I've done is inside me now, forever.

"Angel," he says again, louder this time. I look up at his face.

I don't find anger there, but I can't pinpoint the look he's giving me right now, not with this noise in my head. "I...I..." I slump, trying to get something out, to explain any of it...all of it?

A band comes across my chest and takes me a moment to figure out he's buckled the seat belt and then pulled it tight. Then he wraps my hands around a silver flask.

"Drink this, Angel. It'll help you get back to yourself." He guides my hands, still clutching the flask, up to my mouth. I stare into his eyes as I take a heavy swallow. It's some kind of whiskey, and it burns all the way down to my belly. The heat cuts the cold, firing a path through the chill and the haze. He's right, it helps. This time I take another long gulp without his assistance and cough through the resulting burn.

I hand him the flask and sink against the leather at my back. My fingers are still trembling, but the rest of my body seems to have calmed down.

The SUV pulls away from the light of the hotel, casting shadows across the car. I risk a look at his face. His full lips are set in a grim line, and the stubble on his chin is thicker than the last time I saw him. His hair is messier than usual, as if he's been shoving his fingers through it over and over. The dark waves are unruly but not as crazy as my curls are after days of ignoring them.

I turn my attention out the window and focus on the lights. Now that we are alone together, panic begins to thread through the shock. I called him, and I know I shouldn't have. At the time, I didn't even remember making the call, but something in my head told me he was the best option.

Now, alone with him, anger practically wafting across the back seat, I'm rethinking my choice. I left for a reason, and I'm not sure the trade is worth it. No, I know it's not. The second he learns the truth about his mother's death, I'm dead, his son is dead, and he won't be able to live with himself after that.

In one moment of fear and shock, I've doomed us all.

Something cold touches my cheek, and I jerk backward, bumping my head against the window. He's cleaning my cheek with a wipe he pulled from God knows where. I lean in this time so he can get better access, even as my mind screams to get out of the car and run.

My hands quake again, and he presses the flask back into my hand as he scoots closer, cups my chin, and rubs the wipe harder. It occurs to me he's washing my father's blood from my skin, and I take another long swig of the whiskey.

I don't know if I'm more used to it now or if my mind is just clinging to sanity any way it can, but I don't cough this time. The liquor sinks through me, warming me further. Maybe if I'm drunk, this confrontation will be easier to handle. If I'm drunk, maybe my death will be easier to accept.

When I lift the flask to take another long drink, he snags it from my hands and shoves it between his knees. I let him continue to mop up my face and then move down to my neck in long strokes. I'm dying for him to say something…ask for an explanation, or to unleash his horrible building anger on me so this will all be over.

My father's face, etched with shock and pain, flashes in my head. The gunshot following, then starting again on a loop.

"Angel?"

I blink and look over at him. His hand is still pressed against my cheek with the wipe, his forehead bunched, his eyes searching mine. "You left me for a moment. Breathe, Angel, and it'll pass soon."

Since I don't trust my voice to ask when, I just nod, hoping it placates him for now.

But I don't get a reprieve for long, not that I deserve it. When his hand falls away from my cheek, I know it's time…to explain something I can barely keep straight in my own head. Especially here with him beside me, the heat of him, the scent of him so close. I ache with the need to touch him, but I know I can't. Not now. Not after leaving him.

"Are you going to say anything?" he asks, his voice low and full of pain.

It eats at me. Digging into the already gaping hole of my heart to carve away a little more.

I can't answer, so I shake my head.

"That's all I get? A headshake? What happened to being honest with each other? That's what..." He turns to look out the window and throws the soiled wipe at the back of the seat in front of him so hard it flies back into the trunk space.

In my mind, he finishes his sentence...*that's what made him fall in love with me.* He couldn't bring himself to say it, though, so maybe he's already given up on me and decided I'm not worth it.

My worrying about it is absurd, considering I'm trying to run away from him to end our lives together even though it only just started.

My tears start again, and I swipe them away, turning to look out the window so I can convince myself he won't see.

But he always sees everything. Right through me, into the deepest pits I try to hide.

Again, the vision of my father, but this time a question arises. "Will they kill me now, execute me for killing him?"

He jerks at my words and seizes my chin in his hand, his grip bruising. "Who? Who do you think will kill you? Is that why you left?"

I shake my head the best I can within his iron hold. "No, the council. Will they come after me for killing my father? You're already dealing with them on one front. I don't want you having to face them again a second time. Especially since they both deserved what they got, and you would have never been involved with either of them if it weren't for me."

Tears roll down my cheeks and over his wrist, but he doesn't seem to notice. "Don't you dare take Sal's death away from me. He deserves what he got, and the council will never be able to prove who killed him. Not without the body. As for your father, Kai is very good at what he does. No one will find a trace of him. The council will conduct an investigation, but they won't find anything. Stop worrying over things you have no control over."

His words are meant to calm me, but they don't. Every new death on my hands...Rose, Sal, my father...is another stain on my soul. There can't be anything good left of me.

Adrian gives my chin a little tug, forcing my gaze back to his. "I can see you aren't hearing me. Don't worry about it. They want me, not you. The investigation into Sal's disappearance is only a ploy to take me down. The society loves a good power shuffle, and I know many council members are looking to step into the void."

It seems strange to talk about this now, after everything, and with so much still up in the air. "Are we ever going to be safe?" I whisper.

His grip tightens until I have to pull away from him. He releases me but keeps his eyes locked on me. "I told you I'd keep you safe. You're the one who left, so you put yourself in danger. Something I won't allow to happen again."

I swallow hard and nod. "What do you want from me?"

"Answers, Angel. You have no idea how out of my mind I've been with worry. From now on, you won't step foot outside our bedroom without permission."

His possessive and demanding order is nothing short of how he's been since the moment he claimed me as his own. Yet I have little desire to fight him on it. In fact, I have very little fight left. My exhaustion weighs on my shoulders, pulling me down.

"What do we do now?" I whisper.

He shifts closer and whips another wipe from the pocket of the seat in front of him. "Right now, I'm going to try to get a little more blood off you before you walk through the lobby to the elevator with a wide smile."

He scrubs at my face, probably harder than necessary, but I submit, letting him do whatever he wants. It's not like I could stop him, even if I wanted to.

When he is satisfied, he tosses the wipe on the floor. I expect him to slide back to his side of the car, but instead, he gets closer. "When we get home, you will give me answers. Don't think I'm letting you off the hook just because I haven't stripped you naked and forced you to talk."

The idea of him using sex to wring answers from my heated body short-circuits my brain for a moment. I didn't doubt he could do it for a second. Especially not with the way he's looking at me right now.

I swallow hard, and it's loud enough I can hear it over the sounds of the city passing outside. "So the council isn't going to kill me?" I trust him to protect me from them, but that doesn't mean I'm safe.

He shifts again and rubs his thumb down my cheek gently. "The council won't lay a hand on you, Angel. But that doesn't mean I won't kill you myself. I haven't quite decided yet."

I shiver as I stare into his eyes. His threat sounds more like a promise…and that's only going to get worse when he learns the truth.

8

ADRIAN

*A*s much as I wish I could, I can't kill her. Things would be easier if I could cut her out of my life. Then she can't hurt me, can't be used against me, and can't throw me away like everyone else does.

I settle into the seat beside her and try to ignore how she's shivering. It's the shock, and I've fortified her against it, but there's only so much I can do right now.

When we arrive at the penthouse, I shrug out of my jacket and help her into it to cover the blood splatter on her clothes.

I help her out of the SUV and lift her chin to meet my eyes. "Smile, walk in like it's a regular ole day."

She nods, swallowing heavily. My security knows she went missing, but only a select few. The regular guards aren't privy to everyday household operations. So when my men see us together, I don't want any reason to question our presence. These days, I don't know who I can trust, save my five, because spies are always willing to cross alliances for a high enough price.

I clutch her to my side, and she's rigid, her smile forced and wooden. It'll do since most of my employees are afraid to even look at her too long out of fear of what I might do to them. It pays to be the king.

I lead her onto the elevator, her body still even as she clutches my hand, hers threaded on top of where mine holds her waist.

The penthouse is deserted when we step out of the elevator. She pauses when moving over the threshold into the foyer, her body trembling hard against me a moment, and then she regains control.

I lead her to the bedroom because we are about to have a very violent conversation, and I want privacy.

I release her once we're inside the bedroom, and she stumbles a few steps and then sinks onto a chair in the corner, her head hung, every bright shining thing about her dimmed and dull. Did I do this to her? Or was it her father?

The question remains...

"Why did you leave, Angel?" I try to keep my voice level and calm. Maybe if I stay calm, she will finally give me some answers.

She shakes her head after a few seconds of silence. I curl my hands around the chair opposite hers and resist the urge to throw it across the room. At least she didn't pretend not to hear me.

I stalk around the chair and grab at the elastic in her hair, removing it to let her curls fall around her face and shoulders where they belong. The strands hang dull, dirty, and defiled, just like her.

It eats at me to see her this way, a shadow of the woman I love. If only she'd tell me what's wrong so I can fix it. Take us back to where we were when she met my eyes without fear. Had it only been a couple of days ago? I feel like I haven't touched her in so long...too long.

"Are you going to tell me anything? Or sit there until I force it out of you? I know you don't want me to be that man, but I will...until you tell me what's wrong." I fist my hands on top of the chair and focus on staying steady. I hate this feeling, like everything in me is raging to get free if I don't hear her say something to defend herself, explain her actions.

This cowering sniveling creature is not the woman who came to me all those months ago with a deal. She's not the woman who stripped naked to bare her pain in exchange for a promise.

But now...she has a promise to keep. And I won't give her the option of backing out, not when I've finally held up my end of our bargain. It would have been a cherry on top to get her father too and save her this pain, but maybe one day, she'll be thankful she got to pull that trigger.

I crouch in front of her and force her chin up. She squeezes her eyes closed, and I grip her chin a little tighter. "You are not a child, Angel, so stop acting like one. What is this? What's going on? Talk to me."

She sniffles. "Or what? Will you torture it out of me? Force me to tell you whatever I'm willing just to get you to stop. It doesn't sound like a good strategy."

Bold words from a woman who hasn't stopped shaking since I dragged her out of that motel room.

I shove her chin up and away from me, pushing her back into the chair. "You might think I have a soft spot for you, and you aren't wrong, but I always take what is owed to me. We made a deal, etched in blood, and I've already carried out my end. Your part is simple...you belong to me."

I stand and stalk around the other chair again, keeping the piece of furniture between us. "It's simple. You hold up your end of the deal, and we're fine. If you intend to run the moment you gain any freedom, I'll keep you chained to my bed like a pet."

She sobs, and I don't let it fracture this anger I'm gathering around me like a shield. I've never needed a shield. Not until her. She does something to me, twists me up until all I can think about is laying my claim into her skin over and over again.

"Why are you saying these things?" she whispers.

This time, I do throw the chair. I shove it over and out of my way to get to her easier. Taking her arms in my grip, I shake her. "When I woke up a couple of days ago, I thought I knew my place in the world. And then I came home to an empty penthouse, and my first thought was that someone betrayed me and took you. It didn't occur to me you were the one who shoved that knife into my back. And then tonight you call me, asking for help, and I provide it. All I want in return are answers...and you can't even give me that."

Her only response is to hang her head. Heavy tears beat against her bloodstained jeans in dark dots.

I push her back into the chair again, disgusted. She'd been tortured and left for dead by her fiancé and wasn't this useless afterward. Why is she now? What's happened that she's so scared of me, or of something she's not telling me?

The remaining alcohol in my system is making me tired, but I can't sleep, not while knowing she could walk out that door in the middle of the night.

I stalk around the room, needing to burn off some of this anger before I do something I'll regret. "Why are you just sitting there crying? Why aren't you defending yourself? Yelling at me? Screaming? Anything!" I roar.

She flinches but says nothing. Not a single word to corral or condemn me.

Maybe that hurts most of all? She's decided I'm not worth fighting for, that what we have isn't worth fighting for. But why? I hate that I don't have the answers, and I hate she won't give them to me. Every heartbeat of silence only fuels my rage higher.

This time when I pass the decorative table against the wall, I swipe the top with my arm, bringing the glass and items to the floor in a glittering pile of rubble. None of it matters. I keep my eyes locked on her, looking for a response. Anything other than the crying and the shaking...please.

I walk over the broken pieces to the bedside table and toss the crystal lamp against the wall near her chair. This time, there's not even a flinch. She keeps her hands pressed between her thighs with her chin tucked as tears continue to stream down her face. It's like she's completely alone, and I don't exist on her radar at all.

"Fucking do something!" I yell.

Nothing. Not even a blip of movement from her.

Well. If she won't defend herself or show me any kind of reaction, fine. At the very least, I'll have the respect I'm owed as her husband and as the head of the Doubeck family.

I stand taller, straighten my shirt, and smooth back my hair with both hands. It needs more than I can do for it now to keep it in place, but it doesn't matter when she's not even looking at me.

As I walk back across the room, the glass crunches under my shoes, grinding into the hardwood. I stop beside her chair and place my hand on its back. "You're disappointing me, Valentina. I don't like to be disappointed. You belong to me, and I'm going to ensure the entire world knows it. That way"—I crouch beside the chair, grabbing a piece of broken glass that had skittered near her feet—"if you decide to leave me again, there's not a soul around who won't immediately dump you right back on my doorstep."

She's shaking again, not just her hands but her whole body.

I drop to my knees and turn her chair to face me, the glass cutting into my palm as I move her. Red dots drip to the floor, and her eyes lock on them, staring, her mouth slack. For a moment, she's gone, and I know—God, I know—she's seeing her father's death again. Over and over in her mind. Sometimes, I still have nightmares about my own father's death. But it won't stop me from shaking her awake, demanding the submission she should already be giving me.

"Valentina," I snap. "Focus, Angel." I raise the glass, its glossy red edge sharp and already stained.

Her gaze shifts to the glass and then back to me. I know she doesn't see it yet because I don't even see it. Not really. It's like my body has taken control, my baser instincts to claim on overdrive, especially without a good enough reason from her to leave. Not that I'd ever be able to think of a good enough reason.

I press the shard's point to her exposed forearm, and she freezes with a gasp. When she starts to jerk away from me, I snatch her wrist flat and hold it down against her thigh. "No, Angel. I gave you the chance to talk to me. To make me see reason. Now other needs are in control, and the only thing I want is to mark you, claim you, own you like I deserve."

She whimpers, and I hate the sound from her lips. Even that day I made her strip naked in front of me, she didn't make such pitiful sounds. "Why are you doing this?"

I draw the edge of the glass across her skin no more than a few millimeters. A tiny well of blood clings to the edge, matching my own. "I want to carve you up, put my name on every inch of your body so no one, especially you, will ever forget who you belong to."

I stare down at that drop of blood, mesmerized by the idea of my name there...each letter scarred over and white against her peachy skin. But I keep my hand still, unmoving. It seems even now, with my baser instincts driving me, I can't hurt her that way. Not like her father did, not like her fiancé did.

I'm almost ready to throw the glass away, get it out of my sight so I don't finish what I started, when her hand lands on top of mine.

I glance up into her red-rimmed eyes and stutter out an exhale. There's no fear there...something softer, gentler...that tiny glimmer of the woman I love.

"If this is what you need to do to forgive me, then do it. I can take it. I can take it for you."

9

VALENTINA

"I would do anything for you," I whisper. "Whatever you need."

He brings the shard of glass up to my face, my own hand still clutching his. "Except stay. You'll do anything for me except stay." His voice is a chasm of pain. A reflection of the abandonment he's suffered over and over again in his life—by his mother, his father, and now me.

It hits me that I've only added to his pain. Threaded my own betrayal in with everyone else he's loved in his life. My hand shakes, and I let it fall to my lap so he's pressing the glass into my cheek alone.

"Do it," I say, hoping he can hear the apology in my tone. "Do what you need to do to forgive me."

His eyes search mine, back and forth, dark and unyielding. Every part of him screams to press the point to my flesh and let it bite down. To etch him into me so that it's permanent. More permanent than our wedding vows.

When his hands tremble, the tips of his fingers fluttering against my cheek, he drops the glass. It hits the floor and shatters around our feet to join the rest of the rubble.

He grips my arms tightly, squeezing me together, crumpling me inward like a piece of paper. It's not to hurt me, I can tell by the set of his jaw, but to remind me how close to the edge he remains. If I knew how to bring him back to the light, I would, but I fear I'll never be able to walk there again. Not when so much of me has been stained with blood.

I close my eyes and breathe him in. Even as I feared him hunting me down and finding me…I also feared never seeing him again. Never tracing the edge of his jawline or smelling his clean smoky ginger scent. It's what I thought about when I was alone. That scent. Even now, it winds around my body, calming me in ways I haven't been for too long.

When he reaches under my legs and lifts me, my eyes snap open. But I don't tangle my hands around his neck and into his hair. He probably wouldn't reject me, but if he did, I couldn't bear it. Not after everything that's happened today.

"Easy, Angel. I'm just going to wash you," he whispers. Unlike the first time he bathed me, he starts the shower and walks us both inside, clothing and all. Once under the multiple showerheads delivering delicious hot sprays over my tense muscles, he rips at his clothing. Nothing of the careful, deliberate man is in his eyes now. As if my leaving him has stripped a part of him away. It hurts because I love that part of him.

His clothes make a wet pile in the corner, and I swallow hard against the sight of his erection, bobbing against his stomach as he seizes my waist and drags me forward. "I said be calm, Valentina. I won't tell you again. I'm not going to fuck you in the shower with your father's blood still dotting your skin."

I have nothing to say to that, so I simply nod and let him strip off my dirty clothes. He tosses them on top of his own pile and then scrubs my skin pink with a loofah and his own soap. The ginger scent spirals around us in the water and on our skin. Even the steam carries the fragrance out of the stall. I go languid in his arms, like a doll whose string has finally reached its end.

"Easy," he whispers. Rubbing my back, he rocks me against him. Not sexually, but like a child in his arms.

The fact he's trying to comfort me after what I did to him widens the ache in my chest so much more. I burn with it from the inside out. I feel the shame of leaving him and then not even being able to do it properly, only for him to hold me, save me from ruin all over, and wash between my toes where somehow even blood managed to reach.

"I think you're going to need some new furniture," I say against his chest.

A thread of humor enters his tone. "What?"

"I got blood everywhere. I don't know if anyone will be able to get it out of the car or the chairs in the bedroom."

He pulls away to stare into my eyes. A tiny crease lines his forehead. "You're worried about the furniture?"

Before I can answer him, he's shut off the water, herding me from the shower and wrapping me in a towel. I don't have time to do anything with my curls or do little more than dab off some water as he again guides me from the bathroom toward the bed.

I climb up onto it and crawl over to my side even though it feels wrong to be there while things are still so volatile between us. He wants answers, and eventually, he'll drag them out of me one way or another. It's not as if he doesn't know every single one of my buttons, both for pain and pleasure.

He tugs my ankle, sliding me across the bed on my back, the towel bunching enough to pull free, leaving me naked, spread eagle, and wanting him so badly my stomach aches for it.

Except he doesn't touch me. After he maneuvers me into the position he wants me in, he removes his hands and guides both of them up and down his shaft. "Oh no, Angel, you haven't earned the right to come anytime soon. I plan to make you work for it. If you don't have any answers for me, I don't have anything at all for you."

My fingers tingle, and my stomach roils. Every fiber in my body screams at me to rub my clit and take things into my own hands. But if I do that, he'll be angry. In his mind, it would be cheating. So I ball my fists along my thighs, squeezing the dove gray coverlet hard enough so that it bites into my skin.

I watch him jerk off. One hand reached down to play up my inner thigh, the other pumping furiously while he stares at my nudity. My face burns hot at the intensity of his gaze. I look away until he slaps my inner thigh hard enough to sting. "I didn't give you permission to hide yourself."

I swallow hard and nod faintly, my eyes trailing once again to his erection, clutched tightly in his grasp. He works himself more, faster, his other hand digging deeper into my skin. I don't think he realizes it, nor the fact that I'll be bruised tomorrow. None of it matters as I track a bead of pre-cum leaking from his dusky crown. He gathers it on his next pass, adding it to the water he didn't dry from his body after our shower.

I lick my lips, and he grits his teeth hard. It's almost slow motion as he comes, shooting the white sticky mess across my thighs, my hips, and even a tiny splatter up on my sternum.

Then as I watch, my mouth hanging open, he rubs his spend into my skin, meeting my eyes in challenge until every trace is sticky against my body.

I stay still, watching, waiting while my body is strung tight like a bowstring. It would take him seconds to get me off right now. My heart pounds in my ears, and I'm panting as I squeeze the bedding tighter.

"Stay here, Angel. I'll be right back."

It's on the tip of my tongue to call him back, urge him, tease him into releasing me from this sensual hell. Of course, I don't do it, not wanting to draw his ire further. Soon enough, he'll peel the answers he wants out of me one way or another.

I relax into the mattress, even with my slick thighs and pounding heart. It was a long day. One I can't think about at the moment. Not with everything so fresh. Right now, I need to focus on my future and how I can protect myself when Adrian learns the truth about what I did to his mother.

I roll on my side and curl my knees into my chest, covering my nudity, my shame.

Adrian stalks back into the room, all rippling muscles and elongated gait. He's so beautiful it takes my breath away. I just watch him approach the other side of the bed, then crawl up with me into the mussed covers.

I didn't notice he had something clutched in his hand on his trek in. This time, I recognize it as the tracking gun the doctor used on me after I woke up. It was only months ago, but it feels like years, decades even, since I was that whimpering girl paralyzed in the dark.

He holds it up and turns me by the hip to face him, my head cradled on my arm as I rotate to the opposite side.

"Here's the deal..." he says, loading something in the small device and pressing a plunger at the back. It sort of looks like a hot glue gun, except the tip is sharp and damn painful.

I wait for him to finish his thought.

"This time, I'll put the tracker here." He traces his fingers along the muscled curve of his neck. "You won't be able to remove it without probably killing yourself. I would have done it that way the first time, but it didn't occur to me you'd go back on our deal."

Hot slimy guilt eats at me from the stomach up to my throat. More so for the venom in his tone when he says it.

I swallow and nod. What other choice do I have? If I don't agree, he'll probably kill me and save himself the hassle later. If I do agree, he'll kill me anyway when he learns the secret I've been hiding. There are no good choices here, so I have to take the one I can live the longest with.

I sweep my still wet curls to the side and tilt my head to expose my neck.

He shuffles forward on the sheets, his knees meeting the tips of my breasts as he leans down to find the spot where he wants to do the injection. "Good girl."

I latch on to his bare knee for support when the first pinch of the gun shoots through me. It's over in seconds, and he's leaning back, scanning my face. A hot pearl of blood slides down my neck to land on the bedding, staining it too.

"Are you all right?"

I nod, swiping at the tears overflowing my eyelids. More out of anger and despair than actual pain. It's nothing but a dull ache under my skin. Hopefully, it will be gone by morning. "I'm fine. Can we go to sleep now? I'm so tired."

Without a word, he scoops me up into his arms and walks us across the bed on his knees to lay my head on the pillows. My pillow. Our pillow.

More tears fall, and I can't stop them now. I don't bother trying. Quietly, he uses his phone to turn down the lights.

He gathers me into his arms so I'm pressing my wet face against his chest, the tears falling to land on him. I feel even worse letting him comfort me right now, knowing what he's about to go through when he learns the truth. But I can't give him comfort. Not while I'm at my weakest. Maybe in another day or two, I can gather my strength and try to save all of us again. For now, this is what I need to keep going.

"Angel," he whispers into the now darkened room. "If you leave me again, I will kill you. I won't hesitate, and I won't take excuses."

Fear arches through me, chasing my sorrow. His voice is calm, honed, like the sharpened edge of a blade. One he uses on me with deadly accuracy.

10

ADRIAN

Having her home feels right. For the first time in days, I want to sleep, yet I can't get my mind off the unanswered questions. Why did she run? Where was she going? Who did she meet, and most importantly, who helped her?

She had a cell phone, clothes, food...all things she hadn't walked out of the building with. Clothes maybe, but that's it. The rest she would have had to buy elsewhere, or someone met up with her to assist.

My first suspicion is Kai. But even if he had helped her, he wouldn't have lied to me about it. A little lie to others is nothing, but to me...never. None of my five would dare help her escape, then spend time searching for her alongside me. Especially with Andrea still in precarious health after her attack.

With Valentina's escape, I feel like none of us got to properly process Vincent's death. Of course, he was cremated, as requested, but none of us got to have a drink or tell stupid stories about him. Val stole those moments from me, and it's another thing to add to her ever-growing list of sins. First of which is not answering my damn questions.

I stare down at her sleepy face, resting against the crook in my shoulder. She's perfect like this, a living doll almost. And so young. When you look into her eyes, it's impossible not to feel her life's experiences there. But now, with her pretty eyes closed, she's so fragile and so very, very young.

Marking her with my cum and putting my tracker back under her skin isn't nearly enough to take the edge off my rage. My fingers clench, and I gently ease out of the bed so I don't wake her, then head into the bathroom to grab a glass of water. Even as I gulp it down fast, letting some drip down onto my bare chest, I glare at the doorway leading back into the bedroom.

She thinks she's safe for now, but she has no idea how far I'm willing to go to protect what's mine. She should never have called for my help if she didn't want to belong to me again. I would never have stopped hunting for her, even if it had taken years, but she might have been free longer if she'd run faster, farther, deeper into the dark. But even then...I make my home there, and not even the light in her can keep her safe from it.

I slam the glass onto the counter and head back out into the bedroom. Once I make it across the glass-strewn floor to the closet, I pull on some boxer briefs and step up beside the bed again. After a quick scan to make sure she's fine and still breathing, I weave through the wreckage of our bedroom again and step out into the hallway. Here, the air doesn't smell like her or her arousal—of sex. It's clean, and I take a few deep breaths and head toward my office.

Since it's early, I don't pass anyone as I enter and take the chair behind my desk. I grab my laptop, flip it open, and then just stare...willing myself to do something to get my focus back where it needs to be: destroying the council once and for all.

I stare at the screen a moment longer and then sigh, bringing up the security feeds I'd combed through dozens of times. Each one a link in why Val had left that day. When I left for the council's summon, I didn't think for a second that she'd be gone when I returned. It hurts all over again, a lump in my throat spreading down into my chest. A dull ache I'm not able to dislodge.

Just as I have for the past couple of days, I watch and rewatch the feeds. I didn't have cameras positioned at every angle around the penthouse, preferring to have some privacy, but now, people won't even be able to take a shit without it being recorded.

Keeping them on a loop, I watch again. There's nothing there. At least nothing to give me any kind of answers about why she left or who helped her. I need answers to both questions before I can even begin to reassemble our relationship.

She belongs to me. Her life, her secrets, her lies...all of them are mine. The fact that she's holding things back is another kind of betrayal entirely. One that might ruin us for good if she doesn't meet my demands soon. For now, I'll let her sleep, but we'll start again with the question-and-answer part of our reunion in the morning.

I started to watch again but then stopped with my finger hovering over the button. I'd seen where she walked out of the building and the street cameras, but I hadn't looked at any inside the house except the foyer.

It only took a minute to find a few more cameras that gave me shots of her. Most were innocuous...her going about her day. But one, in particular, made me stop and rewind.

She'd come into my office at some point. Since she'd moved in, she hadn't been in here once, only the command center. Not that I'd needed to keep her away, but it just never came up as most of my time was spent there or with her.

I bring up a few more file backups, the camera in my office that only sometimes stays on. Usually, for meetings, I shut it down. No need for video evidence of some of my activities or anything that Kai or the others might organize in my name.

Thankfully, a file shows for the date she left, and I quickly open it, fast-forwarding to the time which matches the hallway file leading into the office.

It shows her entering the office, flipping on the light, and doing a quick scan of her surroundings. All perfectly normal, until she steps around my desk to study the pictures I keep on a shelf.

For a moment, I glance over my shoulder at the frames and then back at the screen. What made her stop and inspect these? Why now, why today?

I lean in to watch closely. She goes over the pictures one at a time, her fingers trailing over the images. I wish I could see her face and know what she was thinking, but all I can see is her back and her hand from the angle of the camera.

There's a pause as her hand hovers over one of the frames. Then she picks it up and studies it closely, holding it near her face like she's trying to memorize it. Just as quickly, she drops it and races from the room.

I turn and scan the shelf from top to bottom. One picture is missing. I find it on the floor, the glass over the image cracked. It's the shot of my mother and me when I was just a boy, taken very shortly before she disappeared.

Why did this upset her? Did she realize it was my mother and me? Why would that make her run as if she'd seen a ghost?

I set the frame gently back on the shelf, making a note to replace the broken frame. Maybe she thought I'd be upset because she broke the frame with that particular picture. I'd hope she'd know me by now, to know that despite my temper, I wouldn't punish her for such an accident.

I stare at the frame a little longer and then spin to face the camera feed again. Now I have more questions and still no answers.

It's time my angel answers for her actions. I've let her rest from her ordeals long enough.

I flip the light off on my way back into the hall and run right into someone shrouded in the shadows.

The little gasp of pain she lets out tells me it's Andrea. I release her wrists, which I'd grabbed to keep from her toppling from our impact.

She puts a few feet of distance between us. Even in the dark, I can see the yellowing bruises on her skin. She's wearing a dark-colored robe—purple?—cinched tight from throat to toes, yet she still tries to pull her hair over her shoulder to hide her face.

I hold up my hands in surrender, so she knows I won't touch her again. "Sorry, I wasn't paying attention."

"Stop it. Don't speak to me like an invalid."

It's on the tip of my tongue to bite back at her tone, but I know she's hurting, and I don't kick my men when they are down. If striking out at me makes her feel better, I can take that for her and let her use it to heal. "What are you doing up at this hour?"

She stiffens, a shaft of light cutting across her bandaged knuckles. "I couldn't sleep. I'm just going to the kitchen to get a drink."

All my men have apartments, or houses, elsewhere. But they all also have rooms here in the penthouse to use at their will. My five are the only ones who can come and go without special permission. "I'll walk with you."

"No, it's fine. I don't need a babysitter. It's just a drink."

My patience only goes so far. I step closer and lean in. "Watch your tone, Andrea. I know you need to heal and that you don't need to be coddled, but I'll only put up with so much abuse before I bite back. And I always bite to kill."

She ducks her chin. Submission has never been in her nature, and it hurts so badly to see it there now.

"Are you ready to tell me who I'll eviscerate for hurting you?" She, like Valentina, hasn't shared a single detail about her attackers or the attack. So far, the only information I'd gleaned was from the doctor's medical report. And even then, it took some persuading to make him hand it over.

"Not yet. I'm not going to talk about it yet." Her voice is thready, and her tone rushed.

If I thought she held her tongue so she could hunt these men down herself, I might let it stand. As of now, though, she hasn't made a move to leave the penthouse once in the days since her attack. Worse, she won't come to the meetings, nor will she let anyone help her outside of the care I insist on by the doctor.

I step around her, giving her a wide berth so I don't brush against her. "For now, I'll leave it alone, but I won't forever. Get whatever you need done, done because once my own business is handled, we are going hunting."

I don't wait to hear if she will comply or not before I turn and head back to my bedroom. All of this defiance grates on me, and the need to control rises up enough that I'll need to work out or hit a punching bag to take some of the edge off. Or else I'll end up taking my rage out on my men. Like Kai.

Hot stinging guilt winds its way into my chest. Since Valentina showed up, I've done nothing but treat Kai poorly. If he wouldn't fail me, I wouldn't be doing so, but here we are, stuck in a vicious circle.

When I'd pulled up the video feeds, I saw them together in the hallway…him handing her something while looking grimmer than usual. I'll keep that under wraps for now as long as Valentina starts being a little more forthcoming. I already know she won't let me hurt Kai for her sake, so…if I have to, I'll put a gun to his head and force him to his knees.

My angel is going to give me answers whether she likes it or not.

11

VALENTINA

The second he left, it felt like the air had been sucked out of our bedroom. The ruin of our bedroom after Adrian let loose his rage on it. Strangely, even though the décor and glass flew around precariously close to me, not for one second did I feel unsafe. Before...I couldn't even walk into the same room as Sal without the icy fingers of dread creeping up my spine.

I lie on my side in our bed, which still smells like him. My skin feels clammy and sticky, but I don't care. Even the faint throb in my neck reminding me I'm stuck here forever is more of a relief than anything else.

Or it would be. I spread my fingers across my still flat belly. At some point, I'll need to speak to the doctor Adrian seems to keep stashed around here in a closet. Worse...I'll have to tell Adrian and face whatever that flavor of his rage looks like. It's not like I have a choice.

I peek over my shoulder at the clock, an ugly ornate thing I've never liked. Pity he didn't smash that in his redecorating. It's early in the morning. As if reminding me, my stomach lets out a large gurgle. Soon, I'll have to venture out and find something to eat. For now, though, all I want to do is lie in this bed and savor the still lingering warmth his body left behind. The scent of him. The feel of his naked skin against my own.

A shiver rolls through me, and I curl sideways to grab the bunched-up bedding on the floor. Once I shake some glass from the folds, I drag it over my body. It smells like him too, and I inhale that spicy ginger scent of him all over. Gods, I love that smell. I love him. More than anything.

A slippery spiral of guilt worms through me. I left to protect our baby, and I left to protect him as well. Now that I don't have a choice to leave again, I'll have to trust him. Trust that he's stronger than I'm giving him credit for. Trust he's not the monster so many people told me he was when we first met. Not that I've seen any hint of that man since we've been married.

Is he stubborn? Volatile? Overbearing? Of course. But he's never made me feel like a lesser person than him. Never made me feel like he'd hurt me for the enjoyment of it.

Or am I trying to rationalize things out of my own fear? I don't know.

I clutch the blankets into a bunch and tuck them under my cheek, settling into the pillow to think about it more. Just as I let my eyes close, the door of our bedroom bursts open and hits the wall behind it with a heavy thud.

Adrian marches in, seemingly oblivious to the glass littering the floor, despite wearing nothing but his underwear.

Even with his handsome face lined in anger, he's breathtaking.

I sit up, letting the covers fall into my lap. "Be careful. You'll get glass in your feet."

His only answer is to scowl at me. Then he tosses something on the bed and plants his fists down to surround it.

I'm not sure if I'm supposed to look at what he's hovering over or if I should stay still and wait to learn what else I've done to upset him.

"What do you have to say about this?" He stands and waves at the object.

This time, I pull the blankets to get a better look, and my heart stops dead in my chest. Frozen. I'm sure I look as frozen as I feel on the inside too. "I…"

No. I'm not ready to get into this with him. I thought I'd have a little time to prepare, figure out how to break it to him in a way that won't get me tossed out or, worse, killed by his own hand.

While I've never felt unsafe when I'm with him, his temper is lightning quick sometimes. What if he reacts before thinking, and there's no way back?

I swallow hard, trying to get more words out before he starts demanding them. "I…don't know what you want me to say."

"The truth." His tone is calm and even, despite the rigid set of his shoulders and the tightening down his abs. "I only ever want the truth from you, Valentina. I thought I made that perfectly clear."

He grabs the photo and moves it to the bedside table, facedown. I try not to flinch when he climbs up onto the bed beside me. He reaches out, but I can't let him hold me, not with these secrets between us.

I shuffle backward as fast as I'm able, my throat still clogged on the words I need to say. All of them backed up and unable to break free. "I can't…I don't…" I know it's not enough…not anywhere near enough to explain anything to him.

Tears build now and flow down my cheeks. I ball my fists and turn away. I'm so fucking tired of crying. It's the only thing I seem to do well.

"Valentina," he snaps.

Of course, he's expecting my attention, my obedience, but I can't give it to him. Not in this, not yet, at least. We need more time to solidify things…springing this on him would only make it worse.

I'm shaking, and I wrap my arms around my middle as if I can keep myself in one piece by sheer force of will alone. "Can you accept that I'll tell you the truth, but just not now?" I whisper. "I promise to tell you everything but give me a little time to get my bearings."

It's stupid because asking him for mercy is like asking the ocean to stop beating at the shoreline.

"Valentina," he says again, his voice no less of a lightning strike against my skin for the softer tone.

I try to pull away some more, put the width of our very large bed between us, but he doesn't allow it. His hands are on my arms, dragging me back across the sheets toward him before my feet hit the floor on the other side of the bed.

"I told you before, you won't run from me. You won't leave me. And you won't shut me out…in any way," he says as his fingers dig into my biceps.

I barely get a second, and I'm tucked into his lap. My legs go around his hips before I can even think about how bad of an idea it is.

"You don't get to push me away…not when I've done everything you've asked. I've held up this end of our deal, and now it's your turn. You belong to me," he hisses. "You are mine and only mine. To protect, to keep, to give away if I so choose. Remember that, Angel. You are mine. Keep pushing me, and I'll be sure to show you the depths of the ownerships I've purchased in blood."

I swallow hard and tuck my chin. "What do you want from me?"

His fingers lift my face to force our gazes together. "Everything, Valentina Doubeck, everything…and then when you think you've given over every inch of yourself, I'll show you how much more you have to give. How much more I have to take."

I blink at the force of his words. And the way his voice breaks on the end like he is barely holding himself together.

Even under threat, my body molds to his perfectly, as if I were always meant to be right here, aligned against him. Fit together like two pieces of a cracked and ruined whole.

He slides his hands around to my back, his fingers splaying wide to clutch me tighter against him. At least in this position, he can't do much to harm the baby or me. Not without warning. It has to be enough.

"I'm not sure where to start," I whisper, my voice growing stronger with each word. "The beginning is further back than you probably think."

"Take your time. Neither of us has anywhere to be. Tell me everything," he orders. And his tone is nothing less than a dictate. One I have no choice but to obey.

I try not to fidget as I begin. "When I was small, life wasn't so bad. I mean…when my mother was alive. Things at home weren't awful. Even my father wasn't the awful man you knew him to be. But everything changed when she died. It was like her death sucked the humanity out of him. Worse, he blamed me for her death even though I'd been caught in the blast as well. I only survived because she shoved me under a piece of furniture to be rescued by the fire department. The moment they handed me over to my father afterward, I knew he would have traded my life for hers in a heartbeat."

This part isn't so hard to confess. It's not a secret my father hated me. He's known it since we met, and it's not hard to review the facts of my life.

"Go on," he prompts.

I shift in his lap, but he drags his hands down to my ass to press my hips into his harder. Not a position that works well for focus. "Anyway, he lost her, and I lost everything. From that moment on, the only family I had was Rose. Her mother died alongside mine, and she came to live with us since her father was already dead too. But that part doesn't apply to this."

"This? What's this?"

I take in a long breath and blow it out. "Do you remember the story I told you about helping my father kill a woman? When I confessed my sins, you absolved me...saying I was nothing more than a child and can't be held liable for my father's sins."

He swallows hard and nods, no doubt seeing the pattern of things now. At the very least, catching a glimpse of what I'm going to confess to him next.

"I've blamed myself for that woman's death every day since I realized what it meant. You were the first person to tell me it wasn't my fault. I value that..."

"Valentina..." he warns, his jaw clenching tight. "Get on with it and stop dicking around. Say it."

My hands shake as I pull them into my chest. Not that I'll be able to protect myself if he lashes out. "That day I went into your office looking for you. What I found was the answer to a question I've been asking myself for years. Who was the woman that day? Who had I helped my father murder?"

His eyes bore into mine, the depth unimaginable. I can't look away. I can't breathe. I can't think...not until I get the rest of my confession out.

"So now you know why I ran. I'm the one who killed your mother. I'm the one who left you to your father's cruel abuse...It's all my fault."

12

ADRIAN

It's like every fear and failure and nightmare comes spewing out of her pretty little mouth all at once. She says she's sorry enough times that it's all she's mumbling now through tear-soaked lashes and worry-worn lips.

"I'm sorry," she repeats. "I'm so sorry."

If she apologizes one more time, I'm going to lose my shit. I gently ease her off my lap and climb off the bed... needing the distance.

In my head, of course, she was a child and innocent of the crimes she confessed. But as a son and a man who misses his mother every single day, it's so fucking hard to hear.

She's looking at me for reassurance, or explanation maybe. I can't give her that. I can only turn away and survey the broken fixtures littering the room. A fitting environment, considering how utterly destroyed I am now, too.

Fuck. Can we come back from this?

I can't even look at her. The thought makes me want to rage all over again. And this time, the storm might not spare her.

"Adrian?" Her voice is whisper-soft, another contrast to my own roiling emotions. It hurts even more because she uses my name. She never says my name unless I ask her to... or coax her into it.

I don't turn around for fear of harming her or saying something I'll regret later. "Don't. Stay over there, and I'll try to talk about this with you again later."

Her gasp echoes in my head, so much louder than her shocked inhale.

Thankfully, she doesn't utter another word, and I march out of the room, my feet rolling over broken glass. Just to get free.

With nowhere else to go, I head straight for my office. There is a spare closet with some extra clothes. At the very least, I can shove on a pair of pants. Clothing will help if I need to put even more distance between Val and me.

Andrea has gone back to bed. The penthouse is quiet, but inside my head is the opposite. Everything is spinning, trying to realign what I know about my mother's disappearance, my father's death, Valentina's father's death... all of it. But it's too much, especially after hours of drinking, finally getting my wife back, and then only a couple of hours of sleep.

My brain and my body are both on edge. If I tip over, everyone will suffer. Most of all Val.

As quickly as possible, I shimmy into a pair of slacks and a white button-down. Then I shrug into a jacket, grab my shoes, and throw myself into the chair behind my desk. Tiny shards of glass are embedded into the sole of my foot.

It takes several minutes, but I remove each of them and slip my socks and shoes over the wounds. Nothing is bleeding enough to consider a doctor. I shoot off a text to the housekeeper because she needs to clean our bedroom before Val suffers further from my anger.

With a long sigh, I toss my phone onto the desk and take a deep breath. It doesn't take long for a knock to interrupt. Kai steps into the room before I give him permission to enter.

He nods, his suit perfect despite the bruises on his face. "Boss."

"What are you doing up?"

"I could ask you the same thing. Is something wrong with Valentina?"

I shake my head, not ready to talk about what she revealed. Not when it burns down everything I've known for most of my life. "She's sleeping, I think."

If only she hadn't killed her father. I'd be able to do it... get the revenge I'm owed. Right now, I want to punish her, the only member of her heinous family left. Yet she doesn't deserve it. I know she doesn't deserve the rage I want to pile onto her like blanket after blanket to appease this anger.

I shove from the chair and head for the armory. I punch in the code to unlock the door, shove inside the room, flip on the light, and survey my options with practiced ease. If I can't kill a fucking Novak, then I'll destroy the only thing left of the Novak dynasty.

Kai steps in behind me as I select a few things from the wall. When I turn to face him, he quirks an eyebrow, asking the question despite the purple bruising around his orbital bones.

I don't explain as I shove past him into the hallway with my weapons. "You're driving."

We both walk to the garage and climb into the SUV. He figures out my plan the second I tell him the address.

"There's nothing there. Why bother?"

I stack the olive-green grenades in a small tower on my lap, arranging them so they aren't likely to topple off my thighs. "Did I ask your goddamn opinion? No. Fucking drive, or I'll take myself."

His knuckles go white on the steering wheel, and he speeds us out of the garage onto the deserted streets. With sunrise close, we'll have to be quick on this little errand. The closer we get to the house, the easier I feel about this decision. It's what I need. Valentina will agree when she learns what I've done. From the memories she's shared, nothing there is worth keeping.

Kai pulls up to the gate and punches in the code to open it. The house is dark when we pull up to the front door.

Without bothering to knock, I walk right in. It figures a man like Novak would leave it unlocked. He always believed himself untouchable. I chuckle. And fucking look at him now.

Kai dogs my heels, his jaw tight as he scans the halls for any sign of threat. "We'll have to do this quick. I want to be gone before a nosy neighbor makes the first police call. When we get back to the penthouse, I'll call my contact and have them brush it under the rug." Despite his put-out tone, he opens his hand for one of my grenades.

I slide one across his palm and scan the area for a good place to drop it. An RPG was probably the safer choice for this task. But I couldn't deny myself the pleasure of carefully obliterating the last remnants of my enemy's life. Of standing in his home, on his property, and fucking ripping it apart.

The sound of a blast reaches me before the building shakes under my feet.

Shit. Kai wasn't joking about doing this quickly.

I take one look at the kitchen, pull the pin on the grenade, and roll it toward the huge range on the far end. That should take care of things.

I race out of there fast, meeting Kai in the hall near the foyer. With the last grenade, I pop the pin and toss it as far down the long hall as I can. Then we both turn and race to the car.

The explosions blast us hard and send the car rocking. Kai rushes to the bottom of the driveway to the still open gate.

"Stop by the end of the driveway. I want to watch the entire thing fall in on itself."

He huffs but does as I order. We watch together as fire licks out the windows, blackening the exterior, tearing at the roof.

The fire department is no doubt already en route. The police too. "Let's go."

"Home?"

I shake my head. "Just drive for a while. I can't return to the penthouse yet."

"You realize the council will be even more up our asses now. This paints an even bigger target on your back."

What else is new? The council has wanted to unseat me from my father's throne since the day I took it. If they weren't scheming or trying to murder me, well, I don't know what I'd do with my life.

Freedom from their tyranny is a fantasy I can't afford to indulge in. Especially with Valentina, who has become my biggest vulnerability.

We drive around town as the sun rises. I yawn and lean my head against the window. Not to sleep but to rest. This entire night has felt like it would never end. Now that it has, I don't feel better. Destroying Novak's house satisfied me in some ways but not enough in others.

"Home now?" Kai asks as we weave through the morning traffic.

I picture Val, asleep in our bed, her peach limbs splayed across the sheets, her riot of curls decorating my pillows. Even with that image, the rage burns a path inside my gut. I can't go back until I quench this fire. "No, we can't go back there yet. I need more time to get my head on straight so I don't punish her in ways that might ruin us completely. Just keep driving. Or take me somewhere to distract me. Something."

He doesn't ask questions, only keeps his eyes on the road and drives. His ability to know when to speak and when to shut up is always something I've admired about him.

I scrub my hand around the stubble on my jaw and then up through the mess of my hair. With a few swipes of my fingers, I set it in some kind of order. My knuckles are still bloody and broken from the fight with Kai and my rampage around my room.

Shame gurgles in my gut to join the anger there. I could have hurt her last night with all the glass flying around. Even when I want to hate her, I can only think of her safety. Dammit.

The car stops, and I glance out the window. Even in the morning, the lights of the casino are a brightly lit beacon to the decadent and depraved.

I don't feel decadent today… but maybe a little depravity will set me right. At the very least, it'll take my mind off my wife and the many sins she's yet to confess.

13

VALENTINA

*I*t's been an hour since he stormed out. An hour since my words broke something between us. An hour since my life fluttered apart in my lap.

But it's done. The only secret left between us is the life growing in my belly. Maybe after I've given him some time to calm down, the secret will turn into news… something joyful to share after so much misery and hate.

I toss and turn in the empty cold bed. More than my next breath, I want him back. To feel his fingers on my skin, his mouth on my throat, his deep voice whispering against my hair. I want us back.

Light breaks through the curtains on the bank of windows, and I sigh. Looks like I can't even sleep properly without him here. When I sit up, my belly does a little flip-flop that leaves me bent over and queasy. Shit. Not again. Is it morning sickness, or have I just ruined my marriage before it really began sickness? Either way, I think I'm going to puke.

I race to the bathroom, grabbing a towel from the rack on the way to the toilet. I manage to toss the lump of fabric on the tile before my knees hit a little too hard.

Leaning over the bowl, I heave. Every muscle in my body coils tight and releases. When it's over, I'm panting, my hands gripping the edge of the toilet seat to keep myself upright.

When it happens again, I try to brace myself, but it's little help. Once it passes, I lay my cheek on the seat too, all the energy sucked out of me. It's so unsanitary, but I need the support so I don't flop onto the chilly tile. And I know the biting cold against my bare skin won't be helpful.

I heave nothing but my pride into the bowl three more times before it seems to abate.

It hits me that I should eat something. I don't even know how long it's been since my last meal. When I first woke up, before my confrontation with Adrian, I planned to hunt down some food. After he left, all I could do was sink back into the bed and pray for sleep to take me away for a while.

Now, my body reminds me I'm an idiot, and my baby needs food as much as I do. It takes me several tries to stand without my legs shaking. Then I have to face the minefield of our bedroom to reach the closet for clothes.

There's glass everywhere, but I get to the closet without a scratch and grab one of his shirts to slip into. It skims my knees, and I stab my feet into a pair of slippers to complete the look for now. No one will be up yet, and even if they are, I doubt anyone will be brave enough to comment on my appearance. Not today. Not after Adrian's rescue and my return.

On my way to the kitchen, I think about the old cook. She'd helped me and betrayed me. Or she helped me, only to betray me seems more accurate. My father must have bribed her or planted her as a spy some time ago to keep a watch on Adrian and his team. If that were the case, why didn't Kai uncover it? He doesn't seem the type to miss things as important as a spy in his house.

When I reach the kitchen, it's dark. Figures she wouldn't come back here. If she did, it would be suicide, and she didn't seem the type to roll over and take her punishment when it comes for her. If Adrian finds out what she did… it surely will.

Oh well, I can fend for myself without any staff. In my father's house, most of them ignored Rose and me. We had to scrounge for our own food and feed ourselves. I open the refrigerator and study its very well-stocked interior.

My belly does another slow roll, and I consider if I need to get to the sink in a hurry or not. It passes, and I quickly snatch a bowl of fruit and some shredded chicken.

I set my meal on the countertop in front of a stool and pour a big glass of water from the filtered spout by the sink. Now, with the water in hand, I realize how dry my mouth is. I stand by the basin, hips pressed against the counter to guzzle it down fast. It drips down my chin and onto my shirt, but I don't stop until it's gone. Then I grab a refill and sit down to eat.

I eat like a raving lunatic, shoving chicken and strawberries into my mouth at a breakneck pace. It's not until the air stirs around me, sending a chill down my spine, that I glance up to find I've got company.

Andrea doesn't look great.

Not in an, I survived a brutal beating way, but in an, I'm not taking care of myself way. Her usually luscious black hair is dull and limp around her face. Her eyes, still yellow with bruises, are puffy and heavily bagged.

I gasp. She's wearing sweatpants and an oversized sweater. Not that I expect her to bust out the Prada for breakfast, but I've never seen her any less than perfect. At least not since...

I swallow my food and try to give her a smile. "Hi."

She doesn't return it, ignoring me on the way to the refrigerator.

Shoving another bite of chicken in my mouth, I keep my gaze locked on her as if she might explode at any moment. Of the two of us, I'm the far more emotional one. Yet as someone who's been victimized my entire life, sometimes that explosion can be cathartic. Talking about it always helps, and that was how Rose and I kept each other sane. How we survived.

My chest tightens, thinking about Rose and all the ways I failed her.

I won't let it happen again.

Andrea heads toward the exit, but I call out to stop her. "Come here. I want to talk to you."

I don't know if it's the command in my voice, or she really doesn't want to be alone, but to my surprise, she turns around and plops onto the stool next to me. "What?"

"Sit with me, please. Eat." This time, I don't smile. If she's only staying because she sees me as her boss's wife, then I need to be as hard as he can get.

With shaking hands, which I pretend not to notice, she pops the lid on a bowl of salad and digs a fork into the leafy vegetables. We sit in silence and scarf down our food.

I slow things down, so I don't scare her off before I get the chance to question her. Or, at the very least, offer comfort.

When all my food is gone, I shift on the stool only enough to study her. She looks tired, almost like my insides feel right now. So worn down by the world, there's no going back.

"How are you?" I ask, immediately feeling like an idiot. It's the dumbest question I could have asked.

She glares over her bowl and swallows hard. "Peachy." Her tone is razor-sharp. Lucky for her, I've got experience handling prickly tempers.

"You're right. Stupid question. I panicked. How about this… can you tell me who hurt you so I can go find them and kill them for you?"

Her eyes fly wide, and while I meant it more as a joke, I don't hate the idea. At the very least, I could send Kai or Alexei to do the honors.

This new bloodthirst should terrify me or send me into a fit of fear and turmoil, but it doesn't. Killing the men who hurt her so badly seems like a fucking public service.

"You're going to do that all by yourself, are you?"

I shrug. "What's it matter as long as you get their heads in a box at the end of the day?"

She sniffs and sits up to study me. "You sound a bit like your husband, you know that?"

This time, she looks almost impressed. I wait, holding my breath, for her to answer.

"It was two of your ex-fiancé's brothers and one of the council members... Bach, maybe. I hadn't spoken to him before."

I finally breathe and nod once. "Thank you for telling me. I know this is all terrible. You can talk to me if you want. You were there the day Adrian saved me, you saved me, so you know I've been through the same things."

She jabs her fork into her salad hard a few times. "Yeah, maybe. Does it go away?"

"What?"

"The fear. Before, I feared nothing. Now, it's like I wait for them around every corner. As if they will pop out to finish what they started." Her voice wavers like an old record, scratching and breaking on the end.

I want to draw her into a hug, but I know she doesn't want to be touched right now. Instead, I settle for facing her on the stool. "It goes away...with some distance and some time. Be patient with yourself as you heal. Once your body no longer shows the scars, the mental ones can leap up and grab you long after."

She scans my face, but I don't know what she's looking for. After a moment, she seems satisfied and eats another bite of her salad.

I won't fail Andrea like I failed Rose. It's as if the universe is giving me a chance to right my wrongs. If I had left with Rose when she asked me to the night of the ball...she might not be dead right now. We might still be together.

A tiny voice asks if I'd give up Adrian for that. Because if I hadn't gone to that party, I'd have never met him. It's not a reality I want to consider, so I choose to ignore the voice and focus on Andrea. "You should tell him. He hates that you got hurt because of him, and he needs to feel in control."

She jabs her fork into the salad again. This time, the tines scratch against the bottom of the bowl. "No. It's not his fault, and he doesn't get to diminish the role I do on our team because he needs vengeance. He's not the one who got hurt. I am. So it's my revenge to take, not his."

I love the stone-sharpened edge to her voice. Since we started talking, it's gotten stronger, bolder, like the Andrea I remember from before. She can get that woman back again, or she can turn the battered woman into someone even better.

If anyone can get past this and move on with her life, it's Andrea. Especially if she lets her twin help her. But I don't mention it, not when she's only just started opening up to me.

After a long silence, she lets her fork fall into her empty bowl and shoves it across the granite. "Can I ask you something now since you are all up in my business?"

I swallow hard, my food rolling around in my belly uncomfortably. "I think so. But I reserve the right to walk out if I can't answer it."

She tilts her head like fair enough. "Why did you run? We all thought you were happy here."

Involuntarily, I slide my hand across my lower belly, letting my fingers splay low. It's not as if I can feel the baby yet or even a bump at the sign of him, but it comforts me all the same.

Her eyes dip down to my hand and then flash back up to my face. "Oh, I see. Does he know?"

I shake my head once, tucking my chin.

She hops off the stool, puts her bowl in the sink, and ambles toward the door. "Tell him soon, or he'll take it as another secret between you. And none of us will survive another fallout."

14

ADRIAN

I button my jacket and run my hand through my hair one more time. Despite my attempt, I know I look sloppier than I ever have walking through these doors. This is business, and I never let my personal life impede my business.

It doesn't matter, though, since my office has an en suite bathroom, and I keep a few changes of clothes stashed here in case I need to spend the night. At one point, I'd kept a room here, but the security is harder to control with so many people coming in and out every day.

Kai follows me through the locked door down the long corridor that leads to the fighting ring and into the offices I keep there for myself and my men to use as needed. The casino usually runs itself, requiring minimal oversight from me. Kai keeps things going as needed with help from Michail when necessary.

I enter my office, and Kai closes the door behind him. "I thought you could use some work. A few things have piled up. Maybe you can take care of them, and I can take a break for once."

I snort and remove my jacket and my shirt. First, a shower and shave. Once I feel more like myself, maybe a solution will come to mind. Even if it's a pretty fantasy... there are no solutions to your wife having taken part in your mother's murder.

Kai throws his long frame into the chair opposite the desk and pulls a few files to the edge. "I'll be here when you're done cleaning up," he says, already absorbed in whatever he's reading.

I scan the cuts and bruises on his face, and a fresh wave of guilt chomps through my gut. He's always here for me, even when I forget myself and beat him for his loyalty. But I can't apologize. I don't apologize.

The guilt feels heavier by the second. I head into the bathroom, finish stripping, and quickly shower. I took one with Valentina, but at the time, I didn't finish taking care of my usual needs. Especially cleaning up some of the stubble on my chin.

The orgasm I'd had, marking her with my cum, hadn't been satisfying in the least. It had felt more like a punishment than a pleasure. I consider taking myself in hand, but I don't want to leave Kai out there waiting while I beat off. And besides, fantasies of Valentina fill my head, but I don't feel comfortable with them, not while things are broken between us.

What's worse is, I don't know if they can ever be mended, not after what she revealed and what I've done to keep her safe. The council has me in their crosshairs; the bullet is loaded, and they are simply waiting for the final breath before they pull the trigger. When they take a shot, they usually hit the mark dead on.

I have no intention of being their next hit. Nor will I allow Valentina to get on their radar any more than she already is.

I shove thoughts of their assassins coming for my wife out of my mind and finish dressing. Once I'm presentable, I step into the office and survey the stack of papers across the desk. Kai has his own office here, but it looks like he's been using mine for a while.

"What's all this?"

Kai waves the folder toward the files. "Security updates, hiring forms, more security updates. With these fucking hackers running around, we have to outrace them to keep everything secure."

I sit in the chair and grab the closest file. "I don't know what you're talking about. You are 'these damn hackers,' and I bet you design something that will keep everything safe."

Despite the heavy weight of his gaze on me, I keep my head down, reading the file. After arguing with him for months, he's probably shocked that I've said something encouraging.

"I don't have time for that shit. It's not my job to chase down teenagers who are too caught up in their own ego to get an actual job and avoid jail time."

I simply nod and snap the folder shut. As he said… it's a detailed document about installing security scanners to keep weapons out of the casino. "What about the fight ring? Adding anything new down there?"

"No, it's unnecessary with the security on the entry doors. We'll just hire out more guards to monitor those entrances. Besides, anyone coming to a fight knows to expect a little bit of danger. In fact, some of them show up for that edge. Stupid bastards."

There's a soft knock on the door, and I lock eyes with Kai.

"Come in," he calls.

The door opens slowly to reveal a small woman with killer curves and long loose curls which brush her hips. My mind rebels as she draws closer.

"Sir, you called for me," she addresses Kai.

He meets my eyes purposely this time. "She's for you. I thought you might want to blow off a little steam."

I grit my jaw and clench my fists on top of the desk. "What the fuck makes you think I'd want another woman? I'm married."

He glares and leans over to brace his elbows on his knees. "Yes, but shit is crazy right now. You might want to take some of that rage out on someone else…"

The woman flinches beside Kai. Her eyes meet mine, worry etched in every line.

"I'm not going to hurt you. Don't worry about what he's saying."

Kai huffs and shoves off his knees to stand. "You need to get yourself under control. If you won't beat the shit out of me to do it, use her. I paid her well enough that she'll be happy to accommodate any request."

Even though he's staring at me, I don't doubt his message is for her.

He leaves, and I'm left with a stranger in my office, whose floral perfume is so strong it's threatening to choke me. "What's your name?"

She gulps and then spreads her lips wide in something between a smile and a grimace. "Emma. It's Emma."

I wave at the chair. "Sit, Emma. I won't touch you, and you can keep your money. My friend out there is an idiot."

She sits on the very edge of the leather chair like she's ready to bolt. "Well, what do you want me to do then? I can just get under your desk, suck you off…"

I frown and stare at her. "No, I'm good, thanks. As you heard me tell him, I have a wife at home. I don't need your services in that way."

After a heartbeat, she gives a little shrug and then scans the files on the desk. "What's all this? Maybe you need some filing help."

I scan the built-in cabinets on the opposite side of the room. Well, she did already get paid… a lot more than she would be for doing filing work. "Have at it. Maybe you can clear some of this shit off my desk for me."

She eagerly drops the chain strap from her purse and leaves it on the chair. I study her, watching as she reads the labels but refuses to open the folders to discern the contents. Smarter than she looks, this one.

I open my phone and answer some emails. While I've been dealing with Valentina's disappearance, I've let things slide, as evidenced by the mess in my office. It's time to get back to work, at least until the council makes its next move against me.

Twenty minutes later, Emma's standing in front of my clean desk with her hands on her hips. She looks almost proud as she waits for me to acknowledge her.

Kai chooses that moment to saunter back into the office with a grin. Which slips off his face the second he studies the scene. "You used your hooker to do the filing?"

I shrug, still typing on my phone. "I'm not the one who paid her. You did. And I won't be touching any other woman but my woman."

Emma grabs her bag and shifts uncomfortably. "Do you need anything else or…?"

I wave her away. "You can go, but don't tell anyone about this. The last thing I need is the working girls thinking they don't have to work when called."

She bobs her entire body in assent and rushes out of the room.

I close my phone and slide it onto the desk. "I didn't touch a single hair on her head, and still she flees like I spent the last half hour torturing her. I guess my reputation still stands, even after getting married."

I rub my hands over my head, mussing my hair. "I'm ready to go home now. You driving or…?"

"No." Kai braces his knuckles against my desk. "You need to burn off steam, like I said."

I stand and match his pose. "You don't fucking tell me what I need. That's not how this works. I tell you what I need, and then you run off and take care of it. There is no other dynamic here." Though my tone is even and clipped, there's no doubt he understands how close I am to giving him another beating. Deserved or not. Or maybe that's the plan… rile me up enough to take out my anger on him again since I didn't go for his plan A.

"If you aren't going to drive, I'll take myself." I dig around in one of the drawers for a set of keys. Ignoring Kai, I grab my phone and go hunt down one of the cars we keep on-site.

It's a little conspicuous, a cherry-red Corvette, but it'll get me home, so that's all I care about.

When I climb inside, I expect Kai to already be gripping the other door handle, but he didn't follow me this time. I don't know why it makes something in my chest hurt… Is he giving me space because he thinks I need it, or because he's given up on reaching me? Either way, he and I will need to discuss some things soon.

I peel out of the garage, my thoughts already on getting home, into my own bed, and seeing Val. We have a lot to go over, but she's there… waiting… exactly where she should be. I won't give up that gift, even if it's got Trojan stamped across its forehead.

It takes no time to get home. The traffic of the early morning has already dissipated. The guards at the elevators snap to attention, but I ignore them and punch the penthouse button.

For the first time, it occurs to me that maybe Val wants her own house. A place like her father had. Sprawling stone, old woodwork, something classy.

The thought of a home like that makes me feel like a caged animal. I shove my hands in my pockets to keep from fidgeting at the idea. Maybe there's a middle ground. A way to keep everyone I care about safe while not forcing my wife to share her home with my business enterprise. I'd never considered it before.

The elevator dings open, and I step into the foyer. There's no one around, and as I stalk toward the bedroom, I hope the cleaning crew is already finished in there.

When I push the door open, I sigh. It's spotless. Even the bed is perfectly made with hospital corners at the edges.

Val, dressed in one of my shirts, is sitting on the edge of it with something white clutched in her hand.

"Angel?" I cross the room and kneel to catch her eye. "What is it?"

She folds my hand around the piece of plastic, and I glance down at the pregnancy test with a blue cap on one end.

"This is why I left... and we need to talk about it."

15

VALENTINA

He looks stunned. Even more so than the night we met outside the bathroom at the season-opening ball. Not struck by lightning stunned but got hit by a Mack truck and run over stunned.

I swallow hard and wait for him to say something. He clutches the pregnancy test in both of his hands, staring down at the printed words on the tiny screen. I'm shaking, dying for him to speak, to react, anything, because if he doesn't, I might explode from the tension.

I tuck my shaking hands under my thighs and try not to squirm. In my head, I'm praying he understands what I mean by "the reason I left," and it doesn't start an entirely new fight with him. I'm so tired of fighting.

After what feels like an eternity, he whispers, "Angel." His tone holds a note of reverence I've only ever heard in church. Not a prayer, but a supplication.

He finally meets my eyes and slides the test to rest beside me on the bed. His hands curl over my knees and up my thighs to grasp my hips. It puts him in a crouch, but he doesn't seem to mind as he gazes into my eyes. "Why didn't you tell me the minute you found out?"

As much as I don't want to remind him of what I confessed earlier, I still need to explain. "I thought you'd want revenge... that maybe you'd earned the right. But if you killed our baby and me, I feared you wouldn't be able to forgive yourself when you found out." I splay my fingers over my belly and try to beg with my eyes. "I found out I was pregnant only a few minutes before I spotted that picture of your mother. I went into your office that day to tell you and saw it... but it doesn't matter now. If you don't mind, I only have one request?"

He exhales slowly, but I hear it loud in the silent room. "What?"

"Wait to kill me until after the baby is born. I can't have him punished for my sins. Please," I add, just in case he's in a generous mood.

Again, I hold my breath, waiting for a response from him. Any sign of what he's feeling or thinking right now.

After a few seconds, which feel like hours, he shifts over onto his knees so he can press closer between my thighs. "Valentina... is there anything else you're hiding from me? Anything you need to tell me now, so we don't have to keep going through this. Secrets are toxic, as are lies, and I won't tolerate either."

I consider what Andrea told me in the kitchen earlier. Part of me wants to tell him, if only to ensure she gets the revenge she deserves, but I also want to hold the information back if I need more to buy my child's safety.

So, I make the choice and shake my head. "No. I don't have any secrets about my past or our relationship." It's not a lie… but the omission still churns my belly into a burning pit.

He scans my face, up and down, no doubt hunting for the truth. While he's so close, his heat wrapping around me, comforting me, I let myself relax, just for a moment. The scent of him is strong, spicy, and delicious. If I leaned forward only a few inches, I could taste him so easily.

I lick my lips, and he tracks that, too.

As if he can read my mind, he shifts backward and stands. When he turns away, it's like my heart stops in my chest. Is this it? He's going to kill me. Or worse, throw me out? I thought I'd resigned myself to a life without him when I ran away, but the reality was so much worse than I'd imagined. I can't go through it again.

"How did you even get a pregnancy test in here? You said you took it the day you left, so…who brought it to you?" He rounds and pins me with his sharp gaze.

Shit. I'm not going to risk lying to him. Not when my baby's and my life could still be on the line. At the same time, I don't want to put Kai on his bad list any more than he already is. But still, I resolve, Kai is a grown man who can defend himself… "Kai brought it to me. I ordered him to on the conditions of me saving his life, and you giving it to me. He didn't seem like he wanted to if that matters."

He waves at the test on the bed. So innocuous. A few inches of white plastic, yet...it's changed both of our lives completely. "Did he know?"

I shake my head frantically, hands up in surrender. "No, of course not. I didn't want to tell him before I told you. He didn't know, and he didn't help me escape either."

His eyes narrow, and he steps toward me. A hound on a scent. "Who did?"

I've got no problem throwing that old bitch under the bus...not after what she did to me. What I had to do to protect myself. "The cook. She gave me supplies, brought me a phone. It turns out she was a spy for my father...but I don't know for how long."

He drops his gaze, no doubt calculating. "The cook...that explains why she quit suddenly. I tasked Kai to look into her, but she is just one name on a very long list of suspects."

This conversation is not turning out like I'd played it over and over in my head. Though, as I'm not dead yet, well, I suppose it's going well enough.

He shifts closer to me, his dress shoes scuffing the newly cleaned floor. "You knew this whole time?" he says, almost in a whisper, so quiet he might be talking to himself.

I gulp and watch him as if he'll give me a hint to his feelings. I've never been able to read him the way he can read me.

When he drops to his knees where he stands, I jolt. His head bows into his hands, and all I can think about is comforting him. I slide off the bed and crawl toward him. The wood makes my joints ache, but I don't care.

He takes me in his arms the second my fingers slide over his forearm. "Angel, you should never have had to go through this alone."

I cup his cheeks between my palms and smile. "I'm not alone now."

His hand slides down my arms to my hip and then back up to my stomach. He spreads one hand over my belly, the other trapping the back of my neck. "A baby. My baby."

I nod, the sight of him going blurry through a new round of tears. My ears burn, and I try not to start blubbering all over again. "This is what I want. A family. With you. No more secrets between us, I promise."

Reverently, he trails his hands up and wipes the wet from my cheeks. "No more secrets, Angel. On either side. If you ask me anything, I'll tell you the truth, even if you don't want to hear it."

I nod and push up to rest my forehead against his. God, he feels so good, so right in my arms. I'm finally home. "We'll get through this." Somehow, as I say the words, I believe them.

He wraps his arms around me and holds me closer, our bodies locked together. "I hate that we were apart. And that you felt like you couldn't tell me the truth."

I gulp, not wanting to go near any reminders of what I did to him all those years ago, even if I hadn't known. We aren't in the home stretch yet. As much as he wants to trust me, I know it's going to take time. If we force it, things will only get worse. I need to show him I'm not going to leave him again. That I'm staying, no matter what.

His next words break my heart all over again.

"I wish we could go back to the way things were."

I delve my fingers into the hair at the nape of his neck, feeling the soft tendrils, memorizing how his muscles shift against me. There's nothing to say to such a statement, and I don't want to keep crying. So I remain silent, hoping he knows I wish the same thing.

I close my eyes and take another long inhale. If I could make this moment last forever, I would. Just holding him, the outside world can splinter and fall away. He's the only thing I need.

"Angel," he says again. This time, his voice holds a hint of smoke and ember. It takes only a second for my body to smolder under the heat of it.

No. Not like this...not until I've given him everything. Surrendered everything.

I pull away, and he eases his hands around my biceps. "There's one more thing we need to talk about."

His eyes narrow, darkening as his mouth flattens. "Oh?"

I quickly shake my head, pressing my palms flat against his suit front. "No, it's not about me or even us. But it's still something I know that you don't, and I can't let it sit inside me and fester. Or worse, you find out I've known all along and feel betrayed all over again."

The suspicion doesn't clear from his eyes, though, and that's another gouge out of my heart. "What? If it's not about us, then why do you look so scared?"

I gulp. "Rose. You know she was like a sister to me. I watched her get hurt, raped by Sal, used and brutalized over and over again. The entire time I tried to protect her and keep her safe. In the end, I wasn't strong enough. Not even to save myself. I watched it all unfold, and I didn't do enough. But I'm not going to make the same mistake twice."

His tone is clipped. "You're starting to scare me, Angel. Just fucking tell me what it is."

I shake my head. "No, I want to make another deal."

The second the words are out, he drags me to my feet, almost picking me up off the ground completely. "If this is a deal, then I won't be on my knees, and neither will you. Not unless you're begging for something."

I blink at the heat in his tone. Another wave of arousal pours through me. How can I get so turned on in mere seconds with just a few words from him? It seems impossible.

I clench my fists. No, I need to focus and get this all out so we can come up with a solution together.

"What are you proposing, Angel?" He leans in and presses his warm lips to my pulse point. Involuntarily, I wrap my hand around his neck and hold him there.

It takes me another minute to come to my senses. "If you keep doing that, I won't be able to get this out."

He shrugs like he doesn't care, but I know damn well he does. I can't let him distract us both.

I grip the hair at his nape and pull lightly. He comes away from my skin with a little growl. "Angel, you better fucking know what you're doing."

His tone is deep, dipped in dark chocolate, and oh-so-delicious. Fucking hell.

I step away from him, and thankfully, he lets me have a few inches. "I want to make a deal. I know what happened to Andrea and who was involved. She told me in the kitchen earlier when I went to find food. If I tell you the names, you have to let me help you kill them."

His jaw clenches, and I stare him down so he can see how serious I am about this.

"I won't fail her like I did Rose. If I tell you the names, we go after them together."

All thoughts of distance are gone now when he seizes me around the waist and hauls me against him. "I will not put you in danger." There's absolutely no give in his tone.

I wrap my hands around his neck, holding him just as tightly. "So keep me safe then...but I want them all dead."

16

ADRIAN

"Angel, let's pretend, for a moment, you didn't have a complete meltdown after what happened to your father." I carefully word my statement and consider my next. The last thing I need is to spin her right back through her trauma. "I don't know that you have it in you to kill someone unless they are actively trying to hurt you."

She tucks her chin, her eyes taking on an accusatory glint. "Or you. I'd fight to protect you too."

Well, fuck. Something hot slides through my chest. I curl my hands around her hips and pull her tight against me. "Don't say shit like that, Angel, or I'm going to bend you over the bed and make you scream for me."

She gulps, her throat working, as she tries to school her features. Except she's not sure where we stand—which makes two of us. I can see in her eyes how much she wants me, and it makes my blood boil with my contained need for her. However, I have to keep her safe, and pushing her too fast or too soon won't help her ease back into our life together.

That's all I want.

To go back to when she looked at me like I was the sun she revolves around. Now, every glance is a big fucking question mark in my head.

I knead my hands around to her ass, squeezing the firm globes in my palms. Fuck, she feels good like this. Nothing much to hide her body from me except my own shirt.

Her eyes flash to mine, still full of questions but also the lingering heat that always exists between us. No matter what has happened between us, she still wants me, and I have no intention of keeping my hands to myself.

I clench my fists tight, letting my need for her roll through me. Things are different now. I need to be careful with her. Slacking this feeling is something I'll have to handle on my own. She'll only get the pleasure.

I scoop her up by the ass and skim my mouth up her neck even as she lets out a tiny squeak of surprise. Her breath fans against my ear, and her arms wrap around my neck to keep herself steady. God, every fucking time, I forget how perfectly she fits in my grasp.

"Angel, if you aren't up for this, tell me now so I can walk away. Otherwise…" I trail off, letting her imagination fill in the blanks.

"I don't want to stop," she says against my cheek and clutches me tighter.

That's my girl.

I gently set her on the bed. She unwinds from around my neck and uses her hands to scoot backward from the edge. I spend a minute looking at her, all her pale soft skin and gleaming eyes. Everything in her face, from the clench of her jaw to the heavy gulp she takes as her gaze glides down my body, says she wants me as much as I want her right now.

"Lie back, Angel. I want you to touch yourself for me."

Her eyes fly wide, skimming back up to mine. Then her body flushes pink from her cheeks to her knees, and I clench my fists again, needing the ache in my hands to keep me from climbing on the bed after her. "Touch yourself for me. Part your cunt and show me how wet you are."

The gulp she gives me is loud enough that even I can hear it, but then she slides her hand over her belly, between her thighs, and into her panties. I reach up, grab the lace, and tug them down her legs. "Open for me. Let me look at you. You've been feeling guilty about leaving. Let this assuage some of that guilt."

Her fingers glide through her pussy, and she lets her thighs splay wide open, so I get a look at everything. "That's not fair, using sex like that."

I lean over on the bed, bracing my hands to bring my face low enough I can smell the soft musk of her arousal and the scent of my soap on her skin. "When did I ever say I play fair? Now stop teasing and touch yourself like I would."

She arches her wrist to dip her fingers inside herself, then back out to circle her clit. "Or you could get up here and touch me yourself."

If I climb onto the bed, I'll rail her into the covers so hard there will be stitch lines on her ass from the blanket. No, better if I keep my distance until I can touch her with control. "Keep going," I encourage her.

I lick my lips as I watch her, the need to kiss her there overwhelming. But I ignore it in favor of cataloging this moment, this feeling, for when I take the edge off later. Alone.

She sighs and drops her head back onto the bed, hips tipping upward to increase the pressure of her fingers. All I can do is tighten my grip on the bedding and watch. My cock's so hard it's leaking pre-cum all over my slacks. Control is something I know well and something I know I can give her.

Her breathy moan washes through me, and this time, I lean down farther until her glistening pussy is only a few inches away from my face. She's so fucking beautiful it takes my breath away.

Then her fingers still, and she pulls those wet digits away from her flesh to stare down at me. "I don't want this. I want you. Why won't you touch me?"

I clear my throat and swallow the thick knot there. "I just want to look at you right now, Angel."

She narrows her eyes. "That's bullshit. Something's wrong. Do you not want me anymore? Is that it?"

Letting out a low groan, I stand and strip off my clothes, leaving them in a pile on the floor. It takes me a moment to get the courage to grab my cock tight in my fist. There's no way in hell I'll be able to stop once I start.

"Does this look like I don't want you, Angel? All I can think about is sliding into your tight body and fucking you until you scream."

She holds her arms out to me but then lets them drop to the bed when I don't crawl into them. "Then do it. What's the problem? You won't break me."

I shake my head and give myself one slow tight pump. "No. Right now, I feel very much like I'll hurt you, and I can't live with myself if I hurt you or the baby."

She huffs, anger in her eyes now, which takes me by surprise. "My vagina will push out something the size of a watermelon in nine months or so. It can take a little rough sex."

I swallow and lick my lips, giving myself time, at least enough to explain to her what's going on in my head. "It's not about being rough," I say…still grappling with how to explain something I don't even understand about myself.

Her eyes go wide, and she nods while I squeeze myself again, this time letting my short nails dig into my sensitive flesh. A wave of pain is then chased by a wave of pleasure, and I let it wash over me for a moment.

I'm so lost in the sensation that I don't notice she's sat up and shifted closer on her knees until I open my eyes again. "Angel," I warn.

"Angel," she says, pitching her voice low, mocking. Then normally. "You aren't going to scare me off."

Her hands wrap around my dick, brushing mine away. "If you don't want to touch me, fine, but I'm not going to be the bigger person, not when all I can think about is touching every inch of you."

Her eyes scan from my cock in her grasp up to my clenched abs, to my chest, then finally to my eyes. "You are so beautiful to me. Let me show you how much I love looking at you, touching you."

She squeezes me tight, tighter than I've even been touching myself, and I let out a little guh sound above her head. When I risk a peek down at her, she's clenching her thighs together, and it hits me how much she is really enjoying this.

I let her have her way and sink down onto the bed so she can sit comfortably. She settles next to my hip and throws me a sexy grin.

She leans down, removing her hands, and then drags her tongue over the head of my cock like an ice cream cone. I barely have time to let out a strangled gasp before she's lowered her head, taking as much of my length between her lips as possible. It's amazing, but not nearly enough of what I'm craving right now.

Then she lifts her head and gives me an experimental pump in her hands again. "That's better. If you'd let me, I'd have straddled you and done that with my body, but I know you are being testy right now."

Fucking hell. I lie back on the bed and close my eyes. "Testy is not the word I'd use, Angel."

She huffs, but I know she's only teasing me. Once upon a time, I'd have taken it for mockery and reveled in the ensuing punishment. Coming from her, it's loving and full of her signature sweetness.

When she falls silent again, I start to lift my head to stare at her, but then she grabs me tight, her nails digging into the underside of my shaft, and takes up a sharp pull along my cock, from the tip to the base, and back again.

Holy hell. I groan and reach out to clench the sheets so I don't grab her and slide her across my lap where I really want her.

"Don't stop," I order, my tone too sharp, but she only wiggles against my hip and continues her punishing pace.

I'm on the edge and so close to coming when a spear of guilt pins me right in the chest. She should be coming first, not seeing to me like this. I'm about to get up and push her back on the bed, put my face between her thighs and lick her clean, but just as I tense to sit up, she shifts one of her hands to my balls and gives them a gentle but firm roll around her palm while the other continues working my shaft in long rough strokes.

I groan again and cover my face with my hands. "Angel..."

She repeats the motion, and I feel my balls draw in tight as my entire being clenches to come. It takes her a moment to work it out of me, her small hands no doubt tired from the effort, but she doesn't stop, not until the warm jet of my cum slides down her fingers, coating both of our skins.

I'm panting, and I finally open my eyes and shift my weight up on my elbows to look at her. "You should have been the one to come first."

Her eyes narrow, and she shakes her head. "If I wanted to go first, I could have when you told me to touch myself. Get it through your thick skull that touching you turns me on just as much as touching myself. More so even, when I get to see all those careful layers of control get peeled away in favor of pleasure."

I sit up and study her, her hands still covered in my glistening spend. "Touch yourself now. I want you to rub my cum into your body while I watch you finish."

She gulps and lies back on the bed with no defiance in her eyes this time.

No. This look says I've won. And she hopes I'll claim my prize from her body.

17

VALENTINA

I can't say his distance doesn't hurt. But at the same time, I feel like he's coiled so tight that at any moment, his hard-fought control might break, and he'll take me the way I know we're both dying for. Since the moment I returned, he's been toeing the line of his carefully crafted control, and I'm done watching him fight me. He just hasn't figured it out yet.

As much as I want to slick my fingers along my seam until I finish, I want him inside me more. If I have to push him to the edge to make him realize he won't hurt me, then I'll do it.

Instead of taking his orders, I lock eyes with him and trail my cum-coated hand up to my lips and suck my fingers into my mouth. His gaze goes hooded, and his half-erect cock lengthens again while he watches me.

I take my time running my tongue over my index finger, then my middle, and then suck them all between my lips until he's practically panting as he fists the bedding around him. "Angel..." he warns.

This time, I don't mock him because I'm not in the mood for games. The only thing I want is him inside me, filling me, claiming me. We both need it.

I pull my fingers from my mouth and dart my tongue out to lap at my skin like a cat cleaning off the cream. Even after he made a mess all over me, I can still taste my own arousal mixed with his.

When I've licked all of him off my skin, only then do I slowly slide my hand back down between my legs and dip my fingers between my still wet folds. I'm soaked, the evidence of it no doubt gleaming on my thighs for him to see for himself.

He doesn't wait for me to challenge him again. This time, he pounces. It's so fast my hand gets smashed between our hips as I tried to drag it away when he surged over on the bed toward me.

"Why are you pushing me today?" he asks, his lips brushing mine with each word, his eyes searching mine for something only he knows.

I clear my throat, suddenly dry as my heart kicks up in my chest. "I'm not pushing you. I'm hoping you'll realize I adore you the way you are, and you'll accept you deserve whatever pleasure we can give each other, no matter the circumstances."

"You're pregnant," he says, lifting his lips now as if he's realizing it all over again.

I scoff. "Sure, but I'm not suddenly going to break just because I'm growing a human inside me. Women all over the world do it every single day. It changes nothing about our sex life."

Except it does. I can see it there in his eyes. With me pregnant, I've shifted forms from the wife he fucked ragged against his foyer wall to the woman carrying his child, his heir. Suddenly, my being pregnant doesn't feel so much like a gift, but a barrier, another wall that can be erected between me and someone else.

I lift my legs to wrap them around his back and drag him into me harder. He can fucking try to hide behind that wall, but I won't allow it. And I won't allow him to change us when it suits whatever he has going on in his mind that he refuses to share.

Leaning up, I nip his chin, and at the same time, I curl my hands around to his shoulder blades, dig my nails in, and scrape them down his back hard enough to make him arch against me as if he could escape the pain while falling into it headfirst.

The noise he makes shoots straight through me, amping my own need even higher. "You want to fuck me so hard we both see stars, admit it," I say against his chin while he focuses on his now unsteady breathing.

In this position, his cock slides along my body, the head nudging my clit just enough to send a bolt of pleasure through me. I try to rock up against him, but he won't shift his hips or move at all.

No doubt in another battle for control over himself. I'm still not going to give him time to think about it.

I shift enough that I can slip my hand between our bodies, and it takes no effort to ruck upward and sheath him inside me. It happens before he even realizes what I'm doing, and his exhale comes out of him in a whoosh.

It's like a switch is flipped in his mind. He shifts his weight onto one of his elbows, then brings his hand up to capture my neck, his fingers barely grazing the column. "You're pushing me, Angel. If you don't stop, I'm going to push back."

I shift my hips upward, so he slides deeper into me. "Then push back."

His hand tightens just barely, but then he sweeps it around to the back of my neck to control my head as his mouth comes down on mine. His kiss is brutal, hard enough that our teeth clash and scrape at my lips. His tongue sweeps in next, taking control, licking at my mouth until I'm panting with my need for him and causing my nails to dig into his back in earnest this time.

When he pulls his face away, I feel my heartbeat in my mouth, my lips tingling from the assault, and fucking hell, I want more.

I try to lean up to get another kiss, but he cups my neck from the back tighter, not allowing me to raise higher. "No. You pushed, and as you requested, it's my turn to take control." There's a deep husky note to his voice that promises punishment. Finally.

Then he shifts back and slams inside me hard enough his cock hits my cervix. I let out a little, "Oh," and his next thrust is a tiny bit gentler, leaving me gasping as I cling to him. With each new thrust, he wraps his arms tighter around me until he's clutching me to his chest in a bear hug as he uses his abs to surge into my body.

The position shoots sparks along my nerve endings, and everything tingles. I'm so close to coming, but I need a little bit more friction. I wiggle in his grasp to sink down enough to change the angle. The next thrust hits me exactly where I need, and I groan right in his ear as he pounds me into the mattress.

"Yesyesyesyesyesyesyes," I say over and over against his neck.

He doesn't lose his focus, not for a second. Not even when I tumble into my orgasm headfirst while screaming his name.

When I come back into my body, my limbs splayed across the bed, he is still wrapped around me, clutching me to him like a Renaissance sculpture.

I tilt my head to look at his face, which is strained, his forehead bunched up almost in concentration. It hits me that he's still holding back, even after all that.

I curse and reach around to dig my nails into the firm globe of his ass this time, both encouraging his movements and giving him the barest taste of what he needs.

With a shudder, he slams into me one final time as his breath breaks out of him in a rush. Even his thighs quiver between mine. I can't help but feel a little proud of myself after that reaction.

"Feel better?" I ask and nibble on his earlobe.

With a huff, he shoves off the bed to get clear of my body. A chill courses over my skin, and I roll to get a look at him.

His back is to me, and if I didn't know any better, I'd say he's angry right now. "What's wrong?"

He spins to look at me, his mouth set in a grim line. "You pushed me, and I could have hurt you."

I stretch, languid and sleepy. "But you didn't. I'm fine."

"That's not the fucking point, Valentina. I told you what I wanted, and you pushed for more until I could do nothing but give it to you."

Okay. Hold up. I roll to sit on the bed and pull the covers over my nudity. Fighting naked is never fun...unless it's a game. By the set of his shoulders, games are the last thing on his mind. "You're mad at me for...what? Seducing you?"

His expression is hard to read. It's somehow a mix of scorn and anger, but I'm not really sure. Either way, it pisses me off. What we just did is still scorching every inch of my body. In fact, if he didn't look so mad right now, I'd try to entice him into another round.

I wave at him. "Is this our life now? No more good sex because you're afraid to hurt me."

"It's not that simple."

I pull the covers tighter against me, and he scans me from my toes poking over the edge of the bed to my rumpled hair. "I'm calling the doctor in to check on you and make sure you weren't hurt."

It takes everything in me not to throw the pillows at his face. "Do you want me to clean up first, or are you going to have him examine me with your cum still dripping from my body? While you're at it, are you going to have him look at the lines I left on your back and your ass? At least those might be considered actual injuries."

He stops typing on his phone and stalks toward the bed. "Watch your fucking attitude, Valentina. I am being patient with you because you're carrying my child, but keep pushing when I tell you to stop, and I'll have to resort to other punishments."

"Like tying me up?" I hold my wrists together and thrust them toward him. "I don't know, that sounds kind of kinky. I might be into it."

Memories of my arms going numb, of being tied to a bed for days return, and I let my hands fall to my lap. All at once, when I think I'm okay, that I'll forget what Sal did to me, the memories flash in my mind, reminding me I'll never be free of him.

Unaware of my inner turmoil, Adrian huffs out an angry breath and continues typing on his phone.

"I don't need a doctor," I say breezily, trying to grab at my playfulness again. "You don't have to drag him out of bed this late to do nothing but check my blood pressure because we both know you aren't going to allow him to get anywhere near my lady parts."

He blinks and looks up at me like he hadn't considered having a baby means a medical professional will eventually be all up in my business.

I scoot forward, dragging the sheet off me and shoving his shirt off so I'm naked in front of him. When I approach, he steps backward until he bumps into the nightstand. His eyes are locked on my bare breasts, and I don't mind the staring, not with that hungry look on his face.

Then he seems to shake himself. "Knock it off, Valentina. I'm serious. I won't risk harming you or my son. Not for something like rough sex. Not when we can be careful or just wait until you deliver."

I throw my hands up in frustration and spin away, so I don't have to look at him. Because I'm pretty sure I'll say something I'll regret if he keeps giving me the feral look I know he's not going to act on. And worse, if I push him to it, he's going to blame me for his actions.

I don't know if it's the hormones or my reality crashing down around me, but suddenly, I feel very alone. A far cry from the cherished, loving feeling I had before. He doesn't want a partner; he wants an incubator.

When I turn to face him again, his eyes rake across my face only, refusing to dip lower. "Why don't you go take a shower, and I'll get the bedding changed so we can sleep? You need your rest so our son grows strong."

I've about fucking had it. Anger burns through me in a hot sticky wave as I spin on my heel and head toward the door. Before I make it to the hallway, I call back to him, "I hope it's a girl."

18

ADRIAN

The second she's out of my sight, something inside me snaps. No. She won't do this to me again, not while I have breath left in my body.

I heave myself off the bed, still completely naked, and chase after her, grabbing my discarded shirt on the way out. It's not even that I've told her several times she won't leave my side. It's the fact that she is running again. If she thinks she can get away a second time, she's about to face the harsh reality of how far I'll go to protect what's mine.

Despite following almost immediately, she got a good head start on me. I catch up to her in the foyer, but she's stopped in the middle of it like she's wrestling with the fact that she left the room to begin with. I ease up behind her and lay the cotton over her shoulders so she can cover herself.

"Don't," she grits out, almost on a sob. "Don't touch me right now. I'm not leaving the penthouse; I just needed a fucking minute."

She doesn't curse often, but when she does, it feels like a sucker punch to the chest.

"All my life," she continues, "people have made decisions for me. Who I'll marry, what I'll wear, how I'll act, and you know what... they all say it's what's best for me. Every single one of them...even my father, when he saddled me with Sal, said he agreed to the betrothal because it's what's best for me."

I open my mouth to speak, but she cuts in first, "I want to see Rose."

It takes me a moment to process her request, my heart climbing uncomfortably into my throat, making my words harsher than I intend. "She's dead. You can't see her."

Something feral sparks in her eyes. "You think I don't know that? You said you took care of her, so I want to go to her grave. I never got to say goodbye to her. And right now, if she were here, she's the one I'd be running to in order to sort out everything I'm feeling."

I reach out to pull her toward me, but she shrugs from my grasp. I close the distance between us then, pressing her into the nearest wall. If she won't let me touch her, then at the very least, she'll hear me. "You should come to me if you have something to sort out. We are husband and wife. I should be the person you want to fall back on."

She lifts her chin, her jaw clenches. "And I might if you weren't so determined to keep me locked up like a goddamn prisoner. I'm a human being. I made a mistake, and I apologized. I thought you'd forgiven me, but now it seems like you are using this pregnancy as a way to punish me for leaving in the first place."

I slam my hand into the wall above her head, igniting a throb along my palm, and keep my eyes locked with hers. "Do you have any idea what the council—the society—will do to keep my heir from coming into the world? I'm not keeping you locked up as a punishment, but a kindness. For protection."

"That song still sounds eerily familiar. It doesn't matter, though. I still want to see Rose. There are things I need to talk to another woman about that I can't say to you." Then with her teeth clenched, she adds, "Please."

"Andrea is another woman," I say, grasping at straws now.

"Andrea isn't in any shape to be talking to anyone except a therapist or an arms dealer. She definitely won't want to talk to me about my pregnancy."

Neither of us speaks again, and a tense silence stretches taut. A tear slips silently down her cheek, and it's another punch to the chest. Dammit. Hurting her is the last thing I want to do, but I also won't allow her to jeopardize herself or our baby. So I pull out the big guns. "I can't let you leave the penthouse, not while they are riding me so hard about Sal and his disappearance. Not when his family is seeking revenge. On top of that, we'll have to answer questions about your father sooner or later."

Her forehead crumples, and her shoulders slump. Pushing the guilt button wasn't kind of me, but I've never been a nice man. If being a dick means it keeps her safe, then I'll do what I have to every single time.

Then as if realizing my manipulation, her gaze turns hard, and she shoves at my chest. She's not strong enough to move me, not by a long shot, but her fists will leave bruises on my chest from the effort.

"Let me go," she complains, still trying to shove me away from her. "I can't believe you brought up my father, brought up Sal, to make me feel bad enough that I'll give in to your demands. What is wrong with you?"

There isn't enough time in the world to go into that much detail. Instead, I lean in closer, caging her in with my elbows until our faces line up. "The sooner you realize I'll stop at nothing to keep you safe, the easier this will be. Even if it means keeping you safe from yourself. Fighting is useless because it won't change anything."

Her arm sweeps up to push at me again, and in the process, she knocks something off the nearby table. It shatters to the floor around our feet.

A wracking exhale shudders out of her, and she stares over my bicep to inspect the table and the mess. When I think she's about to duck down to clean it up, she leans farther and grabs another object, this time hurling it to the floor close to my feet.

I raise an eyebrow and watch her closely. "Feel better?"

She scowls, her eyelashes still wet from her tears. "What, you're the only one who can throw a hissy fit and destroy everything?"

"No, but if you make me, I'll restrain you until you calm down. Hurt me all you like, but if you do anything to hurt yourself, you'll regret it."

Her chin hikes up, and as she stares into my eyes, another piece of glass hits the floor in a crystalline clatter. "I have no intention of hurting myself. Why would I, when it's so much more fun to hurt you...at least...when you finally let go of yourself and let me."

Her barbs sink deep, drawing blood. My penchant for pain has never been something I regret, but with her, so perfect and beautiful, it feels wrong, out of tune with the symphony her body creates with mine. The pain I crave is a discordant harmony that isn't meant to be played alongside it.

She moves her arm again, but this time, I catch her wrist and twist it behind her back, then the other to match. With both of her hands secured in one of my own, I press her into the wall, trapping both her hands and mine at the small of her back. "What are you doing?" she whispers, her tone no longer laced with the venom she's been spitting for the past several minutes.

I use my other hand to scoop her cheek in my palm and tilt her head back to look into her eyes. "What does it look like, Angel? I said I'd restrain you."

"If I hurt myself, but I told you I don't plan to do that."

I tighten my grip on her wrists until she gasps, but it's not in pain. She's warm, and a hot flush hits her cheeks the same moment she meets my eyes again. "Don't even think about it."

I'm already hard, but I won't push her right now, not when she might take my balls for it later. "We are going back to the bedroom, and you're going to see the doctor. He's going to confirm that you are okay, and then I'm going to feed you and tuck you into bed."

She grinds her teeth together. "I'm not a child who needs to be taken care of." As if trying to illustrate her point, she arches her hips forward despite her earlier warning.

"I never said you were, Angel, but I'm your husband, and it's my privilege to care for you. Let me do this. Men care for their pregnant wives every single day. Many of them find it charming and doting. Why are you fighting me so much?"

She scowls and wiggles her wrists to test my give. "Most men don't have a doctor on staff and refuse to allow their wives to leave their home. You're being overprotective, and while I enjoy that most of the time, right now, all I want is to see Rose."

"Doctor first."

"Then you'll take me to her grave so I can speak to her?"

I give her a noncommittal noise and then accede. "That will depend on what the doctor has to say about your condition."

She rolls her eyes and lets out a heavy sigh. When she stops straining against my grasp, I know I've won. I release her and gently turn her toward the hall so she doesn't accidentally walk over the mess of broken glass.

We enter the room, and I send a quick text to the cleaning staff for the foyer and then to the doctor to join us in my bedroom.

When the old man finally shows up, he sighs heavily. "She is pregnant not sick, you know."

I like the old bastard's attitude. It's the only reason I pay him obscenely well to stay on my staff exclusively. "Do I look like I care?" I wave at Valentina. "Check her out anyway. I want to make sure she is good to go."

The doctor settles beside her on the bed and takes her pulse while I watch, hating every second his hand is on her skin.

"I won't do an exam, but from the naked eye and her vitals, she seems perfectly fine. The same as when I found her earlier."

I wave at her. "Yeah, fine, but she keeps making demands and yelling at me."

Valentina sucks in a breath. "Excuse me? That has nothing to do with the baby."

The doctor considers and meets my eyes. "Hormones likely. They can sometimes make a woman do strange things."

She sets her jaw and glares at us. "My standing up for myself has nothing to do with my hormones or this child. It has everything to do with you suddenly turning into an overly protective brute who refuses to touch me the way we both want to be touched."

I wave the doctor out of the room. He doesn't need to hear this conversation. When I take his place beside her on the bed, she looks like she might shove me off the edge. "I'll touch you any way you like, Angel."

She glares and folds her arms under her breasts. "No. I want you to touch me how you like…and not agonize over it afterward. How do you think that makes me feel?"

I reach out to take her hands, but she shifts her still folded arms away. "No. I don't want to be touched right now. Not by the doctor, not by you, or by anyone. Please, if you won't let me leave this place, then at least leave me alone so I can have a moment of quiet."

It's on the tip of my tongue to snap back at her and give her a piece of my mind, then roll her to her back and fuck her senseless. Maybe then she'll stop yelling at me every five seconds.

"Angel," I begin, intent on trying to mend this fence I didn't even see from my bulldozer.

"No." She looks away toward the windows. "I don't want to talk, and I don't want you to touch me. In fact, no one will until I've seen Rose."

19

VALENTINA

I sleep in a guest room and cry myself into exhaustion. Hell, part of me can't believe he actually let me go. That he didn't enter this room in the middle of the night to drag me back to his bed and pretend to be satisfied with soft caresses and making love.

And it's not even about the sex. Or the fact that he doesn't trust me to know my own mind and body. It's that he won't accept this part of him. There are graves out there, dirt hiding the bodies of men he's killed, but he won't accept that he likes a little pain with his sex and that I can give him that.

A part of him wants me to be the virginal virtuous wife he married, but that girl is gone. Hell, I've shed that skin completely. The woman I am now loves his sharp edges, but he won't accept that part of me either. That he married a woman who can enjoy hurting him that way.

I toss and turn in the gray dawn light, his shirt still wrapped around me, now tangled up in the luxurious bedding. Every piece of me wants to go back to our bed, apologize for what I said, for hurting him, but I can't bring myself to do it. I've never stood up for myself before, but it's high time I started. Especially if he continues this pattern after our child is born.

Well, that's what he thinks, at least. Hopefully, he's starting to understand that we've both changed for the better.

It hurts me that he doesn't realize that. If he doesn't know that he's changed, how can he see that I have?

I shift back into the pillows and try to get comfortable. No matter how this bed feels, it doesn't feel perfect without his warm weight wrapped around me. But how can we keep going on like this? He's stopped trusting himself and me. Neither of us can live like this. I don't want the same kind of relationship as my parents or so many other high society families have.

The image of his hand wrapping around my neck comes back to me in a flash, and I close my eyes, savoring it. Who knows when I'll get that again.

I check the clock, then consider rising to get dressed and find breakfast. To be honest, I'm surprised he let me sleep away from him all night. A tiny part of me is expecting to open my bedroom door and find him leaning against the frame. I don't know. Maybe he realized he'd gone too far in his protection strategy. Knowing him, though, there likely isn't such a thing as too far in his mind.

None of it matters, though, because I'm hurt. Not in the easily dismissible way married couples argue. No, I feel like he's rejecting me in favor of our child, which is utterly ridiculous.

I resettle in the bed and decide against breakfast. Leaving this room means I will have to face him, and I doubt he'll let me walk away from him again. It's probably a cowardly move, but it's not like anyone is here to judge me for it.

I barely think the thought when a soft knock starts at the door.

"Go away!" I shout. It doesn't even matter who stands on the other side. I'm not in the mood to speak to anyone.

It comes again, this time harder and more urgent. "Valentina?"

It takes me a moment to realize Kai is the one knocking, but I still don't want to talk to him.

He calls my name again, and I let out a long huff. "I said go away. If you're here for him, I don't want to speak to you because he's perfectly capable of finding me himself. If you're here for you, I don't think we have anything to talk about." I don't bother raising my voice. If he hears me, great; if not, I don't care. It's not like he'll walk in without my permission. If Adrian found him inside my bedroom, he'd kill him outright.

"You're acting like a child, Valentina," he calls.

It's on the tip of my tongue to call him out for that low blow, but I don't. It actually works. Shame zings through me until I'm clutching the covers up under my chin to hide from it. How many times did my father use that same taunt? It had been his favorite way to berate me.

I'm about to give him a piece of my mind when the door rumbles heavily, and the hallway goes quiet. A flash of fear skitters through me, thinking he might barge in despite knowing how Adrian would react.

But nothing else happens. The doorknob doesn't turn. No one enters.

"I'm not leaving until you talk to me. I'm going to sit right here in this hallway and shout at you through the door until we can have a discussion," he says loudly through the wood.

The sound must have been him sitting down to lean against the door. I giggle at the absurdity of him sitting on the floor in the hallway in thousands of dollars worth of wool.

"Don't you have work to do? I know he didn't send you here to yell at me through my door."

There's a shuffle that makes the door shake. "He didn't send me at all. I'm here on my own."

I snort, even if he doesn't hear it. "Yeah right, because you have nothing better to do than chase after your boss's wife and mend fences." Wonder how that trick would look on a résumé.

There's a long silence, and I hope he's gone. Just when I let my eyes slip closed to go back to sleep, his voice jolts me awake again. "I'm still here. Still not leaving."

With a sigh, I press a pillow over my face to muffle a loud groan. I don't put it past him to stay out there all day until I give him my attention. The problem is that anything I say will go straight back to Adrian.

After a few moments, I decide to let him talk if it will get him to leave me in peace. "What do you want?" I yell louder than necessary.

His response is even and calm. "I want you to think about how Adrian feels right now."

I slam the pillow down on the bed and glare at the door. "Oh, he didn't send you here, did he? What bullshit."

"He didn't. I'm here on my own because I want you to see things from his perspective."

Still glaring daggers through the door, I yell back, "His perspective is that I'm now only useful to him as a baby maker. As for the rest, I'm definitely not talking to you about it because it's none of your business. Just know that it's all very frustrating from every angle. There isn't just his perspective to consider."

The way he says that makes me think again about him saying I'm acting like a child. Then my father springs to mind, and I'm back in my self-loathing circle. All from a few words from a man I barely know. A man whose loyalty is to my husband despite the fact I saved his life.

"You are thinking too narrowly. Did it occur to you that he is scared? That he's so terrified at the thought of losing you that he'd rather lose you in another way to keep you by his side."

Oh, for heaven's sake. "If this is about my leaving again, I promised I wouldn't. And I won't. I only left the last time because I got scared. Besides, I don't have any other secrets tucked away that might endanger me. Fresh out."

He makes an impatient noise, and I glare at the wood again. He can't see it, but it makes me feel better.

"That's not the kind of losing you I mean. Between now and when the baby is born, anything could possibly happen. We are at war with the council, you could have complications, or Sal's family could sweep in to try to take their revenge. Shit could hit the fan in so many ways. He's not scared of you walking away anymore. He's terrified of you dying."

I gasp and blink at the ceiling, my brain rolling over this new fact. Adrian isn't exactly the kind of man who would admit this kind of fear, especially not to the person tied directly to it.

Damn Kai and his meddling. I shove the covers off, grab some spare sweats out of the dresser, shove into them, and then open the door.

To my satisfaction, he falls backward at my feet in his thirty-thousand-dollar Italian suit. "Fine. You said what you needed to say, so you can leave now. I need to get some breakfast."

He eases back up to sitting, his knees bent so his elbows rest on top. "I haven't finished speaking to you yet."

I cross my arms under my breasts and glare down at him, content he can see this one. "Fine, what else do you need to get off your chest this morning?"

His eyes shift down the hall and then back to my face. Yeah. Tell me again how you came here on your own.

I move to grab the door and slam it on him, but he stops me, his big hand bracing against the wood to hold it open. "Wait. You need to understand something before you go off half-cocked and confront him about any of this."

I still glare. It's not like he's giving me a choice about listening to him right now.

"He loves you."

My shoulders slump. "You think I don't know that. Of course, he loves me, or else he wouldn't be doing this."

He blinks, surprise chasing across his features. "But..."

"I know he loves me, and I love him too. But loving someone doesn't mean they don't hurt you. Hell, I know from experience what a loving hand feels like when it's wrapped right around your neck," I grit out between my clenched teeth. "So yes, I know he loves me, and I know he wants to keep our child and me safe, but I'm not willing to sacrifice our relationship for his overabundance of caution."

This time, Kai lets his hand slide off the door, and I shut it gently, leaving him in the hall alone to consider what I've said. If Adrian was listening, then all the better since I won't have to repeat myself later when our eventual confrontation happens.

Climbing back into bed, I snuggle under the covers. This time, I'm warmer from actually wearing clothes. I sigh and let my eyes drift closed again, fighting the pang of longing to have my husband's arms wrapped around me. There's nothing in the world like snuggling up next to him, breathing in the scent at his neck, knowing that he belongs to me and only me.

Some hopeful part of me insists we'll get back there. That I should give him space and time and let him come to terms with everything on his own.

But there's another part of me. The one that loitered under my father's care for far too long. The one that let Rose get slaughtered in my own home. The one that still bears the scars of so-called love.

That part of me knows better. And it knows that I won't let Adrian smother this growing feeling inside me. A feeling that tells me I'm worth living, and I'm worth fighting for.

20

ADRIAN

I don't sleep. Instead, I carefully ease away from her and rush to my office. It takes time and waking people up, but I pay them enough to deal with it. In less than three hours, I have what I need and quietly return to the bedside.

She's still asleep, her curls unbound and riotous across the pillow with one hand cupped under her cheek. I take a moment to stare at her because, damn, she's so beautiful. She'll be even more so when her belly swells with our child, and I can feel it growing inside her.

As I consider how her body will change, I dig in the paper bags around my feet softly, keeping my noise to a minimum. As a kid, I perfected the art of being invisible and silent so as not to draw my father's attention. Those skills serve me well as an adult too.

This time, I don't monitor how long it takes me to ease every item from each of the bags. It could take years, and I wouldn't stop, wouldn't blink, wouldn't be anywhere else than here at this moment.

Once I finish, I sit on the edge of the bed, slightly away from the dozens of baby paraphernalia I've arranged around her sleeping body. When she wakes, I want her to see how serious I am about making this work. About beginning our family together. Will it be perfect? Hell no. But it will be ours, and that's all that matters.

Now that I'm finished, I'm anxious for her to wake, but I also know she needs her sleep. While I waited for the personal shoppers to complete their missions, I read up on the first trimester and what it will do to her. At the very least, the next time she argues about my fussing over her, I can cite sources to back up my decrees.

When she finally stirs in the covers, her shifting knees knocking into clothing and toys, she wakes, blinking into the hazy pre-dawn light. She sees me staring and freezes. "What? What's wrong?"

"Does something have to be wrong for me to admire my wife?"

She frowns, the lines bracketing her mouth matching the one bisecting her forehead, belying her young age. "Yeah, if my husband is sitting on the bed, fully clothed and staring...it definitely makes me think something might be wrong."

I give her a soft smile and shake my head, then deliberately shift my eyes to the item nearest her: a minky, soft gray baby blanket.

She follows my look and lets out a little, "Oh." Then her gaze rakes over the array of items until she sits up to take it all in. "Did you sleep at all?"

I ease up the bed enough to grab her hands in mine. "No, but that doesn't matter. Right now, all that matters is you knowing that I'm serious about this. That I'm excited, even if the news came as a bit of a shock. I'm not going to promise I won't overreact as you progress, but I'll do my best not to burden you with it."

Her features are still drawn up tight as she looks at everything but me. "It's not a burden that you care."

Gently, I tug my fingers from hers and gather the items on the bed. Still sleepy, she reacts slowly, chasing after my hands to catch things before I remove them. "What, wait, stop, what are you doing?"

I can't help but laugh as I tug the baby blanket from her death grip. "I'm putting them in the bassinet for now, don't worry."

She releases the blanket and stares over the edge of the bed. "There's a bassinet? I didn't even see it. Where—?"

I kiss her lips to keep her from talking. Her hands come up to frame my face, as I expect, giving me the room to pull out the jewelry stashed in my jacket pocket. With her distracted, I arrange the diamonds around her hips in a circle and then clasp the largest, the angel wing necklace, around her neck.

She gasps and breaks the kiss to stare down at her bare skin. The blankets pool around her lap, and I take in the sight of her draped in diamonds, bare breasts on display below them even lovelier.

"What?" She gasps and fans her fingers over the bracelets, earrings, rings, and other necklaces I've been hoarding to bathe her in. "Oh my God, where did all this come from?"

I lean in and nibble her lip, trailing my fingers down to gently roll a pink peaked nipple between my fingers. "The jewelry store, my love, as usual."

She huffs and shoves at my chest, a smile playing on her lips now. "Obviously. You weren't worried about all this wealth just sitting around here? I don't need all of this."

Tugging the covers away to get more access to her body, I begin to layer each piece of jewelry on her body until she's glittering in the dim lighting.

I give her a minute to look at everything. She raises her arms and twists her hands and fingers to get a better look. "These are all so beautiful, but really, I don't need this."

If she hasn't learned by now, I get what I want. Right now, all I want is her draped in jewels and nothing else.

I cup her hips and drag her closer to me so I can speak against her lips. "Since when do you have a choice? I bought these for you, and also for me, to see them on you. Not a single stone can compare to your beauty, but damn, do you make them look good."

A faint pink flush rises up her neck and into her cheeks. I ease her hair away from her face, trapping the wayward curls behind her ears.

She lets out a long sigh and nuzzles her face into my touch. "I don't know what to say. Thank you, I guess...they truly are lovely. I've never owned jewelry like this. My fa...well...thank you. It's stunning. All of it."

I know she shifted away from discussing her father, as she probably will for some time. My chest aches all over at how she had to handle that situation on her own. If I'd been there, keeping her safe like I promised, maybe she wouldn't have had to.

The ugly guilt rises, mingling with my still smoldering anger at her leaving, but I shove it away, unwilling to taint this moment with her. This moment when we celebrate the new life she's bringing into the world and into our family.

I lean in and touch my forehead to hers. "I know we didn't discuss it much when we got married, but I've always wanted a child of my own. A baby to erase the sins of my own father, to show light, and love, and joy to."

Her eyes snap open, and she pulls back to meet my gaze. "Our child's life will never be like ours. Not ever. I won't allow it to be raised thinking it's hated or have him feeling like a target." Her voice trembles with her conviction. As if she can say the words forcefully enough to bring them into existence.

But she doesn't need to convince me. Not about this. "He will never, ever feel like we did growing up. I promise you, Angel. He'll feel safe, powerful, and protected every single day of his life."

"What if it's a girl?" she teases.

I nip at her bottom lip, making her squeak backward. "Then she will feel safe, powerful, and protected. But I can't guarantee she'll appreciate it when she gets older, especially when men come sniffing around."

She laughs and cups my cheeks again, her hands warm and firm as they mold to my face. "I'm sure. But Mom will be here to make sure you guys don't get out of hand with it."

Mom. I almost choke at the word on her lips. Mom. Fucking hell, we are going to be parents. It hits me all over again in a wave of anxiety. How can anyone prepare for this and think they are actually ready for the moment?

Her fingers slip down my jaw and curl around the sides of my neck as if she can't keep herself from touching me now that she's started. "You don't know how badly I needed to hear all of this. I never expected you to be the kind of person to hurt a child, but I guess I just needed reassurance. To feel like you know exactly what I want in case something happens."

I jerk and knock her hands away, seizing her arms. "Nothing will happen."

She opens her mouth to speak, but I shake my head slowly. "Nothing. Will. Happen."

This time, she gulps and stays silent until I loosen my hold on her. Only then does she speak, but slowly, as if I might detonate with the wrong word. "Both of our mothers thought they had all the time in the world too. Losing them did terrible things to our fathers."

I snort. "I'm pretty sure both of our fathers were terrible people before they lost them."

"It didn't help to send them in the right direction. I need to make clear that I want our baby to be protected and cherished, no matter what. No matter how you feel if something happens to me."

I swallow hard and meet her gaze, boring into mine. "Nothing is going to happen to you, and I refuse to allow the thought into the conversation. But I hear what you're saying. But what I have that our fathers didn't is my five…they would kill me rather than watch me turn into either of our fathers."

It hits me all over that Victor will never meet my son. His absence I've had to power through is a hole open and aching inside me.

She searches my eyes for a second and then nods, satisfied. There's an edge to her voice when she speaks again. "Good. Not that I want anything to happen to you, but…growing up, I'd rather not have a father than the one I'd been left with after my mother's death. No child should endure that, or the feeling they are worthless to their own parent."

When she leans forward and wraps her arms around me, the jewelry we both forgot about catches on my shirt.

She freezes and stares down at the diamonds again. "I should get this off so I can dress, and we can talk some more. Make plans. I know we have time, but things are volatile right now with the council."

I help strip away the jewels and lay them on the bedside table for her to arrange in her jewelry box later. When she climbs out of bed, I rake my eyes down her bare skin, intent on cataloging any changes. Of course, nothing is different. She looks a little thin from her time away, but I can fix that easily enough.

"Go get showered. I'll put this stuff away, and we can—"

She shakes her head and places her fingers over my lips to stop me from speaking. "I'm not done with this yet. I need a few more things from you to feel safe and secure in our baby's future."

I don't bother hiding my confusion as she lets her fingers fall from my mouth. "What else do you need?"

Isn't it what I promised her all that time ago…she'd feel safe? I haven't kept that promise lately, and it eats at me.

"I want you to promise me that you will protect our child with your life. No matter what happens, he will come first, even before me."

It takes me a second to realize what she's asking of me. Another to dig inside myself…it's hard to promise another's safety over hers, especially someone I haven't met, held, or touched. But there's only one right answer here. "I'll protect our child. But I won't lose you. Those are the only terms I can agree to. If you have a problem with that, then…I don't give a fuck."

21

VALENTINA

I'm not sure what reaction he expects to his proclamation, but I know it's not for me to pull out of his arms, wrap the sheet around my body, and leave the room in a trail of white Egyptian cotton.

His surprise is the only reason I get a head start down the hallway on the way to the command room.

"What are you doing?" he asks from behind me. His silken voice entwines in things I can't allow myself to consider right now, not when I need to finish this.

Despite his protests last night, even I can see he's hesitant with me. Slow to react in whatever way feels natural to him. He's blocking his instincts, and I need it to stop, or we will never get out of this hole we've slid into.

I cast a glance over my shoulder and speed up enough he has to huff and move faster behind me, even if his legs are much longer than my own.

"Angel," he warns as I round the corner into the command room where I freeze to find Kai sprawled in a chair, his tie askew, his legs thrown up onto the desk.

"Don't you dare fucking look at her," Adrian warns, but Kai hasn't so much as glanced our way since we entered.

"Out," Adrian snaps further, but I shake my head.

"No. I need him for a minute."

My husband is practically vibrating with tension behind me. "Excuse me?"

It's on the tip of my tongue to tell him to calm down, but I know how well that works on anyone, so I don't.

I wave at Kai, who remains very still, and absolutely not looking anywhere near us. "This is what I need. I want you to keep that promise preemptively. Set up provisions for the baby if something happens to us."

"Us?" Adrian echoes softly. "I already told you I'm not entertaining thoughts of something happening to you."

"You then," I demand, even as the words carve something out of my chest. He can't imagine me being hurt any more than I can imagine him being gone. But this...this is what I need to feel safe. If our child is protected from the outside world this way, I'll feel much better. Further, I zero in on Kai again, who's still keeping his eyes anywhere but at us.

"I also want Kai to promise if something happens to us, he'll take care of our child."

"What?" both men say at once. Adrian curses, and Kai freezes, looking like he's even afraid to breathe.

"Angel, we need to talk about this first. Before you…"

I shake my head, hiking the sheet up around me. "No, I won't let you talk me out of this, even if you are very persuasive. I need this, and if you're serious…you can take all the jewels you gave me, anything at all…this reassurance is the only thing I want."

He comes around to face me now, sliding his hands up my arms. I can tell he's angry, still vibrating with the need to rage against my declarations, but I can't let him talk me out of it.

And things will only get worse when I say the next part.

I tug out of his grasp. "Let me put on clothes really quickly so Kai can actually speak to me."

He lets me go. I quickly throw on a pair of leggings and an oversized sweater and race back to the command room.

Adrian is sitting next to Kai with his head in his hands. It kills me to do this to him. Especially right after leaving him and making him doubt me, doubt my feelings for him.

I sit in the chair on the other side of Adrian, clasping my hands on the table in front of me.

"Kai will do it," Adrian says, his tone clipped and cold.

I slide my hand across the back of his neck. His hair is getting long, a testament to how worried he's been. Otherwise, he'd be perfect, ready to face any challenge set in front of him. Another pang of guilt hits me.

"Will you turn and look at me, please? The next part is the hardest, and I can't say it while you're facing away. I need you to see my face while I speak. I need you to see me while I speak."

I let him take his time, and he does, slowly shifting his chair to face me, his knees trapping mine between his as if he's making a point, asserting the dominance it's killing him to keep at bay.

"What part is the hardest? Because this is fucking brutal, Valentina," he says, his voice trembling for control as much as his body.

I swallow hard and exhale slowly so he can't hear the shake and tremor in my own conviction. Every word is a test, not of him, but of myself. If I can't stand up to him, a man who has vowed to protect and love me, then how will I ever keep this baby safe from people who actually might want to hurt it. And there are so many people out there who would rip us both apart if they could. The confrontation with my father only cemented that reality for me.

A hot tear slips down my cheeks, and he catches it with a finger, swiping at my face on the other side to stop the others.

"Just say it, Angel, so we can fucking stop having this conversation. I hate seeing you cry. You know that."

I sniff, trying to keep it all in. "With the current climate in the council and with society, I want you to set up a way for me and our child to run if the need arises. But not just us, for you too…a way for you to run with him, or me, whoever has to keep him safe. Kai too," I add belatedly.

He stiffens in front of me, and I know what I'm asking of him so soon after I made his worst nightmares come true.

The room is deathly quiet. I think Kai is holding his breath as hard as I am. No doubt waiting to spring up to protect me if the need arises. I won't, though, if he needs to unleash that terrible anger out on me. Not that I don't deserve every bit of it.

When he draws his hands away from my skin, it's as if he's carved out my lungs and dragged them away too.

It takes a long time, so damn long, for him to say something. But it's not to me. It's to Kai. "Do it."

His voice is so low, and I barely hear it, but Kai immediately goes to work on his laptop. The screen on the wall comes to life so we can all see what he's doing.

He types at blinding speed. His hands fly over the keys, and screen after screen flashes in front of us. I don't understand most of it, but I see banks, passports, money, anything and everything a person might need to start over.

For the first time in a while, Kai speaks up. "You need a way to access this if something happens. I propose the five have this information to be handed to whoever needs it when it's time. That way, no one can access it accidentally."

I snort. The last part is for me, and I realize Adrian's not the only one who feels betrayed by my departure.

But I don't have time to deal with Kai's feelings right now, not with a volcano about to erupt next to me.

He won't look at me now, and I get it. I do. My stomach is in knots, and I can't believe I'm saying all this or doing it. A huge part of me wants to take it all back and say forget it, just to see the dreamy-eyed way he looked at me a little bit ago again. But I know I can't. My mother should have done this for me. She should have protected me this way, knowing how my life could have turned out. Maybe she'd been naïve, but I can't afford to be, not when it comes to ensuring another child isn't harmed the same way I was.

I slide off the chair to kneel at his feet and run my hands up his thighs, but he keeps his eyes locked on the screen, refusing to look at me.

It takes me fisting his shirt to pull him my way before he turns those frozen eyes to me.

"You, of all people, have to understand why I'm doing this. You saw what happened to me. I need to make sure our child is safe. If I don't, then I've failed at the only thing I've ever been given. The only job I've ever had. I won't let it happen."

His thumb traces across my cheek, and something in his face eases. "Angel…" he breathes. "I wonder what kind of force you'd be if your father had seen your potential and made you his heir instead of his burden."

Tears slide down my cheek again. "Then trust me when he didn't. Let me be your partner in this. But first, we take care of our child. It's our responsibility."

For my entire life, I've been the victim. But now, I can no longer afford to be. I let Rose get killed while I could do nothing. Since then, I've gone over and over what I could have done to protect her while I had the chance. The chance being at any single point before that night. I won't be a victim anymore, and neither will our baby. Not while I'm breathing.

He gathers me up in his arms, turning me across his lap. "Angel," he says again in barely a whisper.

I can only wrap my arms around him and cling. Praying he doesn't push me away, not now, when I'm finally doing the right thing.

We stay that way, our bodies entwined, and I don't even care that Kai is feet away. Let him see. Adrian is my entire heart, and I won't let it slip from my grasp again.

His breath is hot against my neck, and his fingers dig into my rib cage like he is waiting to lose me all over. If anything, I need to fix that. Make him see I don't want to go anywhere. Never again.

The room is dead silent, and I realize Kai has stopped typing. I lean away, and Adrian releases me enough to look over his shoulder. Kai is sitting, his hair tousled, a lollipop between his lips. His gaze is intent on the screen above him, so I turn my focus there.

There's a string of text, lines of code, I suppose. Not that I can read any of it.

"It's done," he declares around his candy.

Adrian nods against my neck. "Leave us. We'll talk later. Make sure you speak to the others about it all. I don't want to hear about it again unless it needs to be used."

Kai snaps his laptop shut, sweeps his suit jacket off the back of his chair, and slips out of the room in seconds.

As soon as the door is closed, Adrian lifts me from his lap and slides my ass across the table in front of him. "I hate this, Angel. I don't need to tell you because I'm sure you see it. But I also understand why you're doing this."

I swallow hard about to speak, but he shakes his head slowly, stalling me.

"I know you only want to keep him safe, and that's the only reason I allowed Kai to do it. But hear me, Angel. If you leave again without it being a life-or-death situation, I will kill you myself. Don't put me through that again. I can't take it."

"Never," I promise, wrapping my hands around his neck. "I'll never leave again."

22

ADRIAN

The smile she gives me is worth all the heartache I just suffered in the last several minutes of her explaining what she needs. I dip my face down to nibble at her bottom lip until she's panting and clutching at me. Just the way I like her.

As I press into her, she slides forward on the table to cradle her knees around my hips and lock me in place between her thighs. "You've surprised me," she says, arching her neck so I can skim my lips down the column of her throat.

Between nibbles, I ask, "How?"

Her hands fist in the hair at my nape, her body leaning toward me, arching into every touch I smooth over her clothing. Clothing she is wearing far too much of.

I peel the sweater off her body, happy to find her breasts bare and her nipples at attention for my mouth already. "Mmm...Angel, are you trying to tease me?"

She shrugs all innocent, but her eyes are heavy-lidded while she clings to me, craving my next caress. "Wasn't on purpose. I was just trying to get back here quickly before you and Kai walked out of the room and left me to fend for myself."

"Never." I dip my hand into the front of her leggings and cup her pussy, my fingers sliding along her wet seam. "I'd never leave you to fend for yourself. That just seems cruel when I get so much enjoyment from taking care of you."

She huffs at my playful words, both of us knowing the issues between us right now aren't strictly about sex.

But then she's easily distracted by my fingers rolling over her clit until I pinch it lightly and make her jolt in my arms. "What are you doing?" she asks into my shoulder.

"Maybe after all this pain, I just need to touch you. I need to put my hands on your skin and remember how it feels to make you come apart in my arms." I use my teeth on her neck this time to mark my claim. "I need to know you're real, and you're here, and you're mine."

When she nods, I reach down and scoop the edges of her pants to pull them off and throw them away. She looks so beautiful naked as she clings to me to keep herself upright.

"What about you?" she whines with no real energy.

"You want my clothes off too, Angel, you'll have to take them off for me."

Her hands attack my jacket, then slowly, she works her way down the buttons of my shirt to tug it out of my pants. I watch her face as she reveals more and more of my skin. And I'm not the only one lost to the allure of her flesh. She's clearly mesmerized by every bit of mine. It starts a warm ache in my chest that I rub to try to dislodge.

She dips down to grab my belt buckle and then shoves my pants down my legs to pool at my feet. Not wanting her to stop touching me, I kick them away along with my socks and shoes to leave me just as naked as she is. "Better?"

Her eyes rove over my bare chest and then down to my abs, where she traces each of my muscles with her fingertips. It tickles the lower she goes, and I have to stall her hand before she reaches my hip bones. "Now you're just being mean, Angel."

I let her go to continue her exploration, and she goes straight for my already hard cock as it juts up toward my belly button. When she wraps her warm fingers around the base, I hiss out a breath and squeeze my eyes closed. At the very least, to stay focused on keeping myself in my own skin. Since we married, she's learned how to touch me, how to pleasure me, and she no longer needs instructions to send me straight toward orgasm.

I stop her hand for a second time and then move it to the table, so I get more time to play with her.

There's a pout in her lips at being denied, so I catch her mouth with mine and strip it away. Melting it under the scorch of my tongue roving hers, devouring her mouth until she's whimpering, desperate to get closer to me so our bodies can create the friction she needs.

I nibble her lip, then break the kiss to trail to her earlobes. As my teeth close over one, I delve my hand between our bodies and slide my fingers through her slick core to reach her entrance. She shivers and digs her nails into my shoulders, sending a bolt of pain through my system. It pushes me harder, increasing the pressure of my touch to bring her up to the brink with me. I want her soaking wet before I slide into her pussy and claim her all over again.

"Tell me what to do. How to give you what you need this time?" she pleads softly, her voice barely a whisper. Does she still fear my response?

I take a deep breath and bring her face to my chest, so her lips collide with the muscle. "Bite me, Angel. Do it hard and trust me, you'll be in for a ride."

She rolls her eyes up to meet mine as I stare down at her straight white teeth clamping around my skin. A second later, a shot of pain hits, and I lose my plans. The need to be inside her was too great to resist any longer.

I tug her hips toward me, lining up our bodies as best as I can with the table height, and then ease myself into her heat. She skims the points of her teeth over my pec, and my knees nearly buckle from the sensation. "Easy, Angel. I don't want to go too soon. Let me make it good for you first."

"I'm already so close, please, fuck me. Please."

It's her extra little begging please that pushes me from aware to undone. I tilt her hips enough to get the angle I want and pound into her. In the frenzy, she can barely keep upright enough to bite me, but each one is like a jackhammer to a cracked glacier, sending fissures of pleasure and pain through my body.

I squeeze her ass tighter now, trying to get more of me in contact with more of her, and it feels so good I can barely think through it. She lets out a breathy moan and digs her teeth into my chest again. I can't think or breathe or stop. Nothing will interrupt this now.

I pound into her harder, faster until her legs wrap around my thighs to keep her from bounding back against the table with each thrust. Her cunt squeezes me so tightly I can't focus on anything else. Until she shouts, "I'm going to come. Please, don't stop."

Each thrust is faster, harder until the table itself is sliding underneath her. So I lift her into my arms, cradling her into my body, and carry her to the wall. With her back against the wall, I squat enough to sink farther into her body and then straighten to press deeper, using the wall for leverage.

"Yes!" she screams, her nails digging into my back, her heels digging into my thighs. Each push into her body is a new shockwave of pleasure I ride closer and closer to completion, but not until she finishes first.

"Come for me, Angel," I growl into her ear. In seconds, she's thrashing her hands up and down my arms as her tight sheath contracts around my cock. Fucking hell yes. I keep going, keeping pace through her orgasm, and only when she slumps in my grasp, her body going limp, do I let myself finish, pounding into her one more time, pinning her tight between the wall and my own body.

I'm panting, drawing in as much air as possible, the pleasure spinning out until it slowly fades into a dull ache in my legs, my chest, my thighs, and my back. "I'm going to put you down now, Angel. Can you stand?"

She gives me a dreamy-eyed look. "Stand? Oh, yeah, if I have to."

Gently, I put her on her feet until she gets her legs under her. They wobble like my own, but she keeps herself upright while she clings to my arm. "Can we go back to bed now? Or breakfast. Maybe both…"

I laugh softly. "Both is fine. I'll order breakfast, and you get in bed. I'll join you in a moment."

When I usher her toward our room, mindful of anyone in the hall, I return to the command room and dress quickly, then grab her clothes as well in case she needs them later. Not if I have my way.

Back in the hallway to head toward the kitchen, I almost run down Andrea. She jolts to a stop and then retreats enough to put distance between us.

"Sorry, I wasn't watching where I was going."

She snorts. "The entire penthouse heard why." But she's not mocking me. Her eyes are too solemn, and her response is nothing more than going through the motions, which makes me even more worried about her.

"Are you doing okay? Need anything?"

She ducks her chin, her long dark hair falling forward to hide the bruises still healing on her face. "No, I'm good, thank you. Let me know if you need me to do anything. With everything going on right now, I feel kind of useless."

I reach out to touch her arm, but she flinches away before I can make contact.

"Fuck, sorry," she mumbles and then rushes off down the hall before I can even say anything.

Kai will have to help her get a therapist in here in addition to the doctor. I can't lose Andrea, not this way.

I march toward the kitchen, gather breakfast, then join my wife in bed.

For one fleeting second, I imagine us to be a normal couple enjoying a lazy morning in bed making love, appreciating each other.

Tomorrow is early enough to break the spell and figure out how to keep us all alive.

23

VALENTINA

It takes about a week, but slowly, I stop tiptoeing around the penthouse. It's not that Adrian has come out and said he forgives me, and really, I don't think he'll ever be able to. Even if he says the words and plays the part.

Strangely, I don't feel like I need that forgiveness. It's mostly because Adrian won't say a single word about it, unlike the man who raised me. My father used to rub every slight back in my face.

I quickly learn the others are slower to forgive, especially once they learned about my condition. Michail, with his quiet intensity, refuses to speak to me. Kai, when he does speak now, mostly uses a chilled tone I don't recognize from the perpetual flirt of a man I'd come to know. But it comes and goes, like he remembers a little to late that I betrayed his best friend and boss. Not that he's ever risked flirting with me. But I saw it all too well the last time Adrian dared to take me out of the house.

That's become my problem now. Adrian refuses to take me anywhere or allow me to leave his sight longer than a few minutes. As much as I love his attention, it's hard being his sole focus because having Adrian's concentration is like being choked to death with the softest silk on the planet. You're not sure if you want to run or ask for more.

I sit in Adrian's office today while he works quietly at his desk. They'd moved an oversized chair that swallows me whole into the corner, and I have to admit it's the most comfortable piece of furniture I've ever sat on.

This is how I spend most of my time now. If not in the command room, I'm always only a few feet from him and no more. Some days, it's thrilling—like when he lifts me up on his desk and orders everyone out—and other times, it's boring.

Today, I'd rather be bored.

Kai came in moments ago and set a DVD and a summons on Adrian's desk, and now we all stand around staring at them as if they will bite.

My first thought is…this is the beginning of the end. The council always wins. My father said that so many times, and at some point, I started to believe it. But this time, if the council wins…it means I lose.

I lose everything.

I won't let someone else, another man, take everything away from me again.

I grab the DVD off the desk, drawing everyone's attention, then stalk to the command room to start it up.

Kai and Adrian follow a few seconds later and do nothing but stand silently seething at my back.

I snag the remote from the table and hit play. The video begins immediately, and it takes seconds to figure out what we are looking at: Andrea's attack.

Bile rises in my throat, and I cover my mouth as the scene progresses. She's beaten and still fighting. Fighting so hard.

Kai makes a noise and turns his back to the screen. Adrian does the same, but I don't. I watch. Not because I want to see it, but because someone needs to witness her bravery. Someone needs to acknowledge she fought as hard as she could, and it hadn't been enough.

Something in my chest hardens. Those bastards need to be ripped to shreds when the time is right.

It takes two hours. Two fucking hours of white-knuckle gripping the table beside me and imagining all the ways these men should pay for their crimes. The final screen is a close-up shot of Andrea's face. I turn around with still clenched muscles long grown sore to look at Kai and Adrian. They are vibrating with rage, and I can see the need to release it in their eyes.

"You see a victim," I say, shaking my head, "but I see a fighter. You might be angry but imagine how angry she is. This is her revenge. You won't take it from her."

Adrian starts toward me and lowers his voice to a deadly whisper. "You won't give me orders in my own home, Valentina."

I square off with him, knowing that he won't hurt me even this angry. "No, I don't want to give you orders, but I can see you both calculating how to get revenge for this. But it's not your vengeance to take. It's hers."

He waves at the screen. "The attack was on her, but this…fucking video is for me. It's a taunt for me, not for her." He lifts the envelope and throws it back on the table. "It was even addressed to me."

I slide to sit on the table, my legs shaking so hard I can't stay upright. He can yell at me all he wants, but I'll never stop defending Andrea's right to go after her own attackers. If I'd been stronger, I would have done the same.

I hear her high heels just in time to lunge off the table and block the doorway. She comes up short with over a foot of height on me. "What…the hell?"

I spread my arms across the entrance and shake my head. "Private meeting."

Her forehead bunches, and she crosses her arms. "Are you in charge now? Have you killed Adrian and taken over without any of us noticing? Considering how far Kai has been up your ass recently, I don't think that's even possible."

I barely flinch at her tone, and I don't blame her. She's been in attack first, ask questions later mode since everything happened. "No, he's in here with me, just slower to get to the door."

Her mouth twists in a macabre smile. "Stop playing around, Val, and let me in."

I set my jaw and shake my head again. "Sorry."

Her eyes rove my tear-streaked face, and no doubt she sees the pain in my eyes. Except she mistakes my sympathy for pity.

"Get the hell out of the way, or I'll move you," she snaps.

I hold firm, and she shoves me hard at the shoulders before I even register she's put her hands on me.

Stumbling back, I land on my ass in the middle of the room. Adrian is in her face less than a second later. "What the hell is your problem?"

The only reason he hasn't hit her back is because of what he just saw. Hesitation is his own form of sympathy, but again, she doesn't take it that way. This time, she goes for Adrian's throat.

Kai finally steps in and gets her in a hold in less than a second. She goes frantic, her eyes wild, her body jerking and fighting against this. But it's not the carefully disciplined moves she learns every day but the fervent dangerous, formless fight of the trapped.

"Let her go," I say, getting to my feet, my hands stinging from scraping on the floor.

As usual, no one listens to me. "Let her go," I say again, this time placing my hand gently on Kai's forearm. Everyone freezes, and Adrian hauls me back.

It takes a minute, but Kai relaxes his grip, and Andrea scrambles out of his hold, shoving him away. "I don't know what the hell is go—" Her eyes finally snag on the screen, and she knows.

She knows.

"You..." Her breath shudders out of her. "You saw it?"

She folds her arms around her middle, and I want to comfort her so badly. Adrian refuses to let me go, no matter how much I try to squirm from his iron grasp. Right now, she's dangerous. A cornered creature looking to claw her way back to reality. I know both that cage and that border intimately.

I turn in Adrian's grasp to meet his eyes. "She won't hurt me. When she pushed me, she probably didn't realize I'd go down so hard. She needs a friend, and I'm the only female in this house who can help her get through this with her soul intact."

He smooths my curls away from my face with one hand, his fingers gentle but unyielding. His eyes hold a million questions and a million answers, but he gives me one sharp nod and then releases his grasp.

I approach her slowly, hands up in surrender. "It's okay. We are the only ones who saw it. No one else."

A choked sob escapes her throat, and she turns away to stifle any more that might come out. I give her a minute before skirting wide to look at her face again. "If anyone knows what you're going through, it's me. We already talked about this, remember? What you see on my face now, it's not pity, it's anger...it's sympathy...it's the need to drive a knife through those bastards' hearts and then keep them alive long enough to feed them their own dicks."

I clamp my mouth shut, a little surprised at my own thirst for violence. Her eyes lock on mine, wary but surprised too. "I don't want them to see it. They will think I'm weak."

Gently, I cup her elbows and steer her to avoid seeing the boys or the screen. "No one who watches this could say you are weak. Not in a million years, not after how you fought, and how you survived."

Her shoulders slowly inch away from her ears, her long dark hair shifting around her with the movement. "I want revenge, I do," she whispers. "But I'm not strong enough to get it yet. I can't leave this damn building for fear of seeing one of them and not being ready to face it all."

I want to hug her so badly, but Andrea is definitely not a hugger, so I keep my distance. "That's okay. You take as long as *you* need. No one will make a move on these pricks until you're ready. Hell, and if you're never ready, I know five very powerful men who would love nothing more than to handle it for you. I promise, if you say the word, they will deliver each of these asshole's heads on a pike."

She drags her gaze from mine over to Adrian, then Kai, and back. "Okay. I believe you."

I nod, satisfied she's not going to do anything stupid that will get Adrian riled up again. "Do you want to tell them about it or talk about it at all yet?"

Frantically, she shakes her head back and forth. I run my hands up her biceps slowly, back and forth, trying to soothe her. "Okay. Okay. Don't worry about it, all right. It's fine."

I stalk over to the table and hit the button on the DVD player to remove the disc. Then I slide it into the paper wrapper we found it in. When I'm standing in front of her again, I wrap her hands around it. "Kai, I'm sure, will try to see if there are any digital copies that can be destroyed. This belongs to you, but if you can, try to keep it in case we need it for evidence."

She chokes out a sob. "Evidence to present to who? The same council who did this to me? No. But I'll keep it for now in case it's needed."

I nod, and she turns away, shoving between the men to get out the door. They let her go but follow her with their eyes until she's out of sight.

Adrian focuses on me again, something new written in his features. "Angel..."

I shake my head and grab the paper, the summons as Kai called it, and hold it out to him. With a grimace, he snatches it and unfolds the edges to scan the sheet. His fingers tighten around the top and bottom, and then he waves it over to Kai, who takes it next.

"What is it?" I ask, stepping into his open arms now. The strength that kept me going for the past couple of hours seems to drain out of me bit by bit after the confrontation with Andrea.

Kai sighs and carefully sets the paper on the table. "It's a summons all right and a threat. It seems the council is content to go to war with us, officially."

"Me," Adrian corrects, his chin pressing into the hair at my crown. "The council wants me, and I plan to give them exactly what they want."

24

ADRIAN

The threat was issued to me, and Andrea had already paid the price of being in the council's crosshairs. I won't risk the rest of my men as well. Not with stakes this high.

I don't sleep much over the next couple of days, so much so that Valentina comments on it when she catches me staring off into space for the third time in the morning. "Are you going to tell me what you're thinking?"

I wave my fork at her, the one I didn't even remember I held. A piece of melon dangles from the tines. "I'm thinking I need to find somewhere safe for you and the others to go."

Her forehead scrunches up as she chews her own food. "The others?" she echoes.

"Andrea is already hurt, and I won't risk anyone else. I'm going to find somewhere safe you all can hide out until this blows over."

She laughs, short and sharp. "If you think they are going to leave just because you order it, then you haven't been paying attention. Every single one of them wants revenge for the attack Andrea suffered and for the council's continued targeting of you. Even with them on your back, the five aren't going to go anywhere, not without you. Especially without you." She narrows her eyes. "Isn't that what you pay them for anyway? To keep you safe."

I hum in my throat. "Among other things," I hedge. She doesn't need to know the extent of everyone's specialized skills.

I snag my phone off the table, finally setting down my fork, and thumb out a quick message to Kai and the others. At the very least, I need to try to get rid of them. My heart tells me that Kai will be the hardest of them to shed. Maybe if I task him directly with Valentina's safety.

I glance over the edge of my phone to my wife, who is happily eating a bowl of fruit while reading the newspaper spread across the table. It'll be hard enough to get her to leave me as well. Especially after we've finally gotten through our disagreement about my protectiveness.

A few minutes pass, in which I shove my breakfast away and settle back into my chair to wait. They file in quickly enough, Kai following Andrea with a heavy frown and Ivan leading at the front.

Victor's absence hits me all over again. Combined with Andrea's attack, I've barely had time to process it. I miss my friend.

I swallow a heavy lump and study them all. Michail, tall and serious. Kai, my second-in-command, dressed perfectly as usual. Alexei and Andrea, so similar yet so different. Finally, Ivan, whose anger is always at the forefront these days. He's a powder keg I don't want to be anywhere near when he erupts.

I fold my hands on top of my stomach and try for nonchalance. Not that it will work, but I have to start somewhere. "I have a special job for all of you. I need you to be ready to go within the next couple of hours."

I catch Kai's grimace from the doorway. No doubt he's waiting for the arguments as well. When no one speaks up, I glance from face to face.

"What do you need, Boss?" Michail says, surprising me, and Kai as well, by the look on his face right now.

I study each of them and lock eyes with Andrea. "Are you good to go, or do we need to put you in a safe house until we are on the other side of this?"

Her glare could cut a lesser man down in seconds. I weather it and nod in return. "You are on Sal's family but don't make any moves. Your afraid to see them, so that's all you'll see until you can look the bastards in the eyes and know they don't own you. But it's strictly a monitor, assess, and report back to Kai. For now."

Something unreadable passes over her features, then she spins, and leaves without a word to anyone else, even her twin, who watches her walk out with a grave expression.

I shift my focus to him for a moment. "You're on the casino. No one goes in or out without you knowing who they are. Make sure everything stays smooth while we deal with this."

Unlike his sister, he gives me a brief nod, and then follows his sister's exit.

Kai clusters closer to Ivan and Michail, no doubt waiting for his own orders. Next up, I pin Michail with a look. "You are on the safe houses. We need to secure what we can and know if any are compromised in case we need to make use of them."

"Do you want them ready with food or just the basics?"

I consider having one prepped for Valentina, but I won't tell him right now. Not when she can hear me and try to throw down again about my protection. "Just the basics for now."

He leaves next, and then I survey Ivan. Of all my men, he's always been the biggest question mark. One minute, he might be perfectly calm, and the next, he's curb-stomping an asshole for sitting too close to him. "Can you handle the business side of things other than the casino?"

"Anything you want me to watch out for?" he asks.

I glance at Kai. "Give him a list of who to keep an eye on when you have time."

Kai dips his head in agreement and then watches Ivan stalk out of the room. When I meet his eyes, he shakes his head. "Don't even think about giving me some bullshit job to send me away. You need someone at your back whether you want help or not."

"I also need someone to ensure Valentina gets out safely if the worst happens. You are the only person I can trust to do this. The only one who has complete control over what we set up for her, besides her."

Valentina clears her throat from the end of the table. "Right here, guys. You don't need to talk around me like I'm an inanimate object."

We both glance her way but continue talking. No doubt she'll have something to say about it later, but by then, I can strip her down and spank her for the impertinence to make myself feel better about it.

Kai turns his focus back to me. "If things are that bad, then she'll be fending for herself from that point anyway."

He has a point, but hearing it out loud doesn't make me feel better. Nor does the thought of my angel out there alone at the council's mercy.

I lock eyes with him. Things have been contentious with us lately, at least on my end, yet he stays by my side when I know he's gotten better offers from other society members. "Is there anything I can say or assign you to do that will make you go?"

Kai leans across the table and pours himself a glass of orange juice, his hand steady as he raises it to his lips. "Nope. I'm not going anywhere." Then he tosses back the juice in two big gulps and sets the glass on the table again.

Valentina makes a noise on the other side of him. "Please, help yourself."

I smile and shake my head, happy for the bickering since it means we might be getting back to normal, at least in the family. Outside of it...well, they have a shitstorm coming that I don't think they are prepared for.

"Since I'm not going anywhere, Boss," Kai emphasizes, shoving his hands into his slacks pockets, "what do you want me to do around here to help prepare us?"

The way he says "us"...like he's in this for the long haul makes me break out in a cold sweat. I can't lose him any more than I could lose Valentina.

She saves me from having to give an immediate answer by drawing his attention. "Have you heard anything about my father's disappearance, or his estates, his money? Any of it?"

Kai shakes his head, a soft look in his eyes as he gazes her way. It's not sexual but sympathetic, and that's the only reason I don't shove him out of the dining room and slam the door in his face for it.

"Nothing so far. There are, of course, investigators looking into his death, a lot of rumors, but nothing that comes back to you or Adrian. And there hasn't been any mention of transferring assets to you or anyone else. They have his will, though. Do you know what's in it?"

She shrugs like she doesn't care, but I see the rigid set of her shoulders as she does it. "No, but it doesn't matter. I don't want anything from him anyway. If he did leave me something, I'm going to give it to charity."

Her eyes stay locked on her bowl as she shifts her remaining food around with her fork. The forlorn look on her face makes me want to gather her in my arms and comfort her all over again. No matter his betrayals and how things ended between them, I think she always hoped he might come around and love her. What little girl doesn't want her father's approval?

Kai glances at me, asking if he should say something, but I shake my head. "Keep an eye on the others and have someone on every single council member. I want to know if they breathe in our direction. Otherwise, stay on the task I gave you before."

As if relieved to get an assignment, he shuffles out the door quickly. I watch him go, hoping this isn't one of the last few times I'll get to talk to him.

I stare at the top of her head from the way it's ducked down, her curls a riot around her face today. "Are you ready for this, Angel? I'd just as soon put you on a plane to some beach island and leave you there until everything blows over."

She huffs and then glares, setting her fork beside her bowl now. "Do we need to go over things again? I'm not going anywhere, especially not with you and the others in danger."

It's the answer I expect since she's been giving it to me nonstop since I got the threat from the council. "Fine. But I'm going to keep asking in case you change your mind."

She dips her head. "Fine. I'm going to keep saying no in case you change your mind."

I lick my lips and shake my head at her. Mouthy little brat.

When I stand and come around the table, she tracks me all the way to her side. "Can I help you?"

I kneel on the carpet and shove her thighs open to make room for me. "I think you need a reminder of who is in charge here."

She arches a perfect dark brow my way. "You're the one on your knees."

I lean down and deliver a bite to the inside of her thigh, right below her panty line. She shivers in my grasp, so I do the same to the other side. "I may be on my knees, but this isn't submission. It's authority."

She leans back in the chair and settles her arms along the rests on either side of her. "Authority, huh? What's that look like?"

I nibble her skin again, drawing a moan from her lips with each small nip. Even though she just showered, I can smell the soft musky scent of her arousal with her pussy so close to my face. I lean in and kiss her over the soft cotton of her panties.

Her breathy moan rocks through me, and my cock goes hard against my slacks. "Sit back, Angel. Let me show you how I own your sweet little pussy."

She moans again when I tongue her slit through her panties. "This belongs to me. I'm only kneeling to get a better taste."

Her fingers delve into my hair, mussing it, but it doesn't matter. Not when she starts begging, proving my point for me.

25

VALENTINA

Despite the cold shoulders I received after returning, I'm happy Adrian got everyone to clear out. The penthouse is too quiet, but I'm proud he's taking care of his people above himself. He might not realize it, but he's a far better person than he likes to pretend to be. We certainly are rubbing off on each other and not just sexually. I've made peace with the fact that I'm going to help take down Andrea's attackers. With my own two hands if I get the choice. Doing so almost feels like justice for what Rose and I endured. I wasn't strong enough to take the vengeance I deserved back then.

Now I can be the woman Adrian needs at his side, and I can care for his people as if they are my own family. Which, I suppose they are now.

I wander the penthouse halls, not really in search of anything, more for the exercise. Adrian is likely shut up in his office, or the command room with Kai, trying to come up with a solution that leads to the least bloodshed. While I agree in most aspects, not when it comes to the people responsible for Andrea's attack. I've been crystal clear on that fact to both my husband and Kai. Lucky for me, they are in complete agreement. I don't care if taking them down escalates things. They deserve to be—I try to think of the worst punishment imaginable—drawn and quartered...if that was still a thing.

After my third lap through the halls, I head back to our bedroom and climb up on the bed. The sheets are rumpled since Adrian has removed all staff, save some of his most loyal guards. He says it's to mitigate betrayal in our ranks, but I also think he does it to protect them. Regular cleaning crew and kitchen staff have no stake in this fight. Another pang of pride zips through me at the thought.

The worst part about this is I feel pretty useless. There's nothing for me to do against the bureaucracy and posturing right now. Especially with Adrian refusing to allow me any freedom outside the penthouse.

I settle back into the pillows, leaning up against the headboard. There has to be something I can do. I've been racking my brain, trying to come up with anything that might be useful, but so far, I've come up empty.

My only advantage is knowing the ins and outs of Sal's family operations. All of which I already shared in great detail with Kai and Adrian in one long sit-down interrogation. If they can use it, I'll be glad. I've wanted to scrub every detail out of my brain since the first moment I learned what those bastards trafficked in. Bile rises in my throat at the resurgence of memory.

Sal showing me the videos he took on his phone of his latest shipments.

Sal crowing about his latest underage conquests.

Sal getting off watching my revulsion.

And his family is just as bad. It takes me a moment to pull out of the flashback, ground myself in the present, and remember I'm no longer in that reality.

As I come back to myself, an idea slips through the fog. At first, I shake it off as a dumb idea, but the longer I let it take up space in my head, the more it starts to grow on me, especially if I'm safe about it. Potentially, I could deescalate everything quickly if it works. But if Adrian found out, I don't know how he'd feel about it, let alone Kai.

I grab my phone off the bedside table and maneuver to my old accounts. This phone has been scrubbed clean, and I need to find an old contact I'd long since happily washed away.

Once I do find it, though, I stare at the screen and frown. This is probably such a dumb idea...but if I don't try, I won't feel like I did everything to mitigate the damage that is coming. Damage that is mostly my fault, to begin with. If I hadn't made the deal with Adrian, we wouldn't be here now. Also, I'd likely be dead.

I hover my finger over the call button for a full minute before I hit send. Even as the phone rings on the other side, I want to take it back, hang up, and pretend I didn't do this.

A gruff voice answers, and I freeze, my hands shaking. I'd heard that voice on countless of Sal's videos. Hearing it directed at me sends a shiver down my spine. Sal's father, Nigel, is not the forgiving type, and no doubt he blames me for his son's death. On the same token, he also doesn't allow personal matters to interfere with business, so at the very least, I've got a small chance of making a negotiation work.

"Hello?" Nigel says again, his tone even more impatient the second time.

I steady my phone with both hands pressed against my ear. "Hello?"

"Who is this?"

Of course, he wants to know who I am, and no matter how I look at things, honesty seems like the best option. "Valentina Novak or rather, Doubeck. Valentina Doubeck." I wince, hoping the correction isn't like waving a red flag in front of a bull.

"What do you want?" His tone is laced with disgust, reflecting my own.

I square my shoulders even though he can't see me and try for the cold and unyielding tone my father used when he discussed business with society members. "I have a business proposition for you."

"Oh?"

I swallow hard, hoping he doesn't hear it through the line. "You get the council off our backs, and I'll make it worth the effort on your part."

He makes a noise that I can't discern. "We should meet face-to-face, girl, and discuss this sort of thing in person. It's the proper thing to do."

I want to tell him I don't give a shit what is proper. I'm not going near him. Instead, I say, "No, thank you."

His answering huff sounds a little like a laugh. "What are you offering?"

Technically, I don't have a single thing to give him, but even I know admitting so isn't good negotiation tactics. Instead, I flounder a bit, then say the first thing that pops into my head. "Money. I can offer you money."

"Money, hmm…"

This time, I cover the mouthpiece as I take in a few nervous breaths. I hold steady and don't respond, waiting for him to say more.

"I'll help you out of this, girl, but it will cost you."

"How much?"

This time, his laughter is dark, and it turns my stomach. "Twenty million, and I'll take care of your little problem."

If he could see me, no doubt, he would have witnessed the blood draining from my face. He's insane if he thinks anyone can pay that for doing nothing more than calling off his dogs. I can't even counter the number since it's so unreasonable.

But I try anyway. "How about one million and an agreement no one will come after your family for the atrocities you committed to one of ours." It's a down and dirty lie since I want all of them dead, Sal's entire family, but he doesn't need to know that. Adrian doesn't like when people lie, but in this case…he might forgive me.

He laughs outright. "Girl, that woman was never yours, only your husband's. Ask yourself why he likes to keep such a pretty woman around. Well, that's probably obvious since you were never much to look at."

I pull the phone away from my face and glare at it. Fucking bastard. Just because I wasn't fawning over his son and his family, suddenly I'm ugly. No. He's just trying to get a rise out of me. Along with his taunt about Andrea. I'm pretty sure both of them would rather gouge their own eyes out than sleep with each other.

"One million is my only and final offer."

"Ten million," he snaps, his breathing husky.

Gag.

Knowing what they will do with that money and who they will use it to buy, I can't do it. I splay my fingers over my belly and shake my head. "No. One million is all I'm offering."

"You called me, girl, not the other way around. I'm perfectly content to watch the council snuff out your entire lot. I'll gladly sweep in, buy up the pieces, and destroy any legacy your husband might have left." He spits the word husband like it's something gross in his mouth.

"I'm not going to give you ten million to buy and sell more children on the black market. I just won't do it." I don't need to explain myself to him at all. By this point, I should just hang up. I knew this was a bad idea in the first place. Except I had to try. For Adrian. For our family.

He laughs again, and then I hear others laugh. Of course, he's had me on speakerphone this entire time. They are all probably huddled around having a good laugh about my groveling to make a deal.

It doesn't matter. I'll sacrifice my pride to keep people safe if I have to. It means nothing to me anymore.

"I think we are done talking," I say, keeping my tone light and calm.

"See you soon, girl," he growls into the phone.

I hang up and lean back into the pillows again. During the call, I'd sat up, intent on listening closely. I hadn't even realized.

There's a soft huff from the door, and I glance up to lock eyes with Adrian. His face is solemn, his eyes gentle as they meet mine. And for a second, there's pride there.

Then he's gone again, the doorway dark. I wrap my arms around myself and whisper a prayer of thanks that Sal's family didn't take my offer. Now, when they all die, I never lied to anyone. I won't have that deceit on my soul.

Just their blood.

26

ADRIAN

No matter what I say or do, I can't convince Valentina to run off and lay low either. She is determined to see things to the end with me. While I'm tempted to throw her on a plane and force her away, I don't think she'll ever forgive me if I did. And if by some miracle we make it out of this thing alive, I plan to live a very long and happy life with my wife. Which will be made easier by the fact she doesn't hate me.

Right now, I'm trying to figure out how to ensure her safety because the council will no doubt try to use her against me. At the very least, they will threaten her safety to ensure my compliance—more like my confession, if they have their way.

It's been two weeks since the summons, and the day is approaching quickly. I sit in my office, leaning back in the chair, my feet propped on the edge of the desk. My life is an aching hole right now without my people around me, and I worry about everyone's safety. Feasibly, I can only worry about my own and

Valentina's, but it's hard not to keep adding people to the mix the closer and closer they get to me.

Val walks into the office in a pair of jeans and a crisp white T-shirt. Like something out of a cleaning ad on TV. I drop my feet and give her a quick sweep with my eyes. "How are you feeling? Okay?"

She sits on the edge of the chair even as I ache to have her walk around and fold herself into my arms. "Nervous, I think. Not sick, though, if you're asking about the baby." Her hand automatically goes to her belly as if she can feel him growing there already.

I keep scanning her body from her head to her toes, looking for differences, but she looks the same. Her hair is still a beautiful riot of curls inviting my fingers to touch. Her body is still perfectly curved to fit my own.

"There is one thing we should talk about?" she says, drawing me away from my thoughts.

"Oh?"

"They are going to demand my presence at some point, right? At the very least to threaten you with. I feel like we need to update my wardrobe, make sure I fit in with you guys and look the part. Most of what I've stocked in the closet is soccer mom chic. Comfortable, but doesn't exactly scream sophistication."

"Do you think it will help?"

She shrugs, tugging on the edge of her T-shirt. "I don't know. At the very least, it might help me play the part I'm supposed to play.

Might help me tap into the feral creature I heard Kai call me the other day." She laughs, but it doesn't reach her eyes.

"He wasn't insulting you or else…"

She waves my concern away. "No, that's not what I'm upset about. I just worry about you, and I don't know what to expect. Things are starting to be okay again, and of course, something has to come along and ruin it. I'm starting to think I'm not built for happy endings."

I heave out of the chair, skirt my desk, and hold out my hand for her to take. "Let's go shopping, Angel."

As we leave the penthouse and head to the car, Kai following close behind, I think she's relieved to be outside. While I fear exposing her to the opportunity for kidnapping or worse…she seems to need this.

It only takes a few minutes to maneuver the traffic and pull up outside a little boutique I've frequented many times. On the way, I texted to ask them to clear the place out and close for us. The privacy will make us both feel better.

I leave Kai in the car, and we both head into the shop, locking the glass door behind as we enter.

Tricia, the shop owner, melts out of the decorative curtained alcoves to lead us back to the dressing room salon area she sets up for her VIP clients.

I don't bother waiting for her to ask what we want but launch right in with orders. "Coffee and tea for us, please. And bring us everything you have in her size. Then leave us to choose."

As if she's accustomed to strange shopping habits, she gives us a little nod and heads out to her inventory with her assistants.

"This is so weird," Valentina whispers beside me, her hand tucked tight into my own.

I lead her to a long gray couch against the far wall, unbutton my suit jacket, and sit. "It might be weird, but it definitely adds a bit of fun to something that can be very boring."

Her forehead wrinkles in that cute way I love when she's thinking hard. "I never really got to go shopping a lot. My father only really splurged on new clothes when they were going to be seen by important people."

I get a little pang in my chest and squeeze her fingers for a moment. "You can buy anything you like, and I won't be shy about insisting you buy anything I like too."

Her gaze flashes to mine as her cheeks redden. "Not here," she whispers loudly.

I chuckle and lean forward as one of the shop assistants deposits a tray on the table in front of me. Without a word, she goes to find her boss and leaves us to our own devices.

"Tea?" I ask, offering her the tiny porcelain cup, already knowing she'll want it.

She gently grips the glass and cups the saucer from underneath. "Thank you. Although, I wish I could have coffee right now."

"Do you want me to pour a cup?"

She shakes her head. "No, I want to hold off on caffeine for a while, at least until we get the all clear from the doctor."

"From everything I've read so far, you can have up to a certain amount per day," I say, pouring some milk into my own coffee.

She stiffens beside me, and I glance at her. "What?"

"You've been reading up about pregnancy?"

I try not to be offended by the surprise in her voice. "Why wouldn't I be researching? I'll be a new father just as much as you'll be a new mother. Besides, it's my privilege to care for you right now, and I intend to do an excellent job of it."

Tricia and the others return carrying stacks of items and laying them out on the tables her assistants cart in. "Is there anything else we can do for you?"

I shake my head. "We've got it from here. Please don't disturb us until I text you again."

They all flee the room and close the curtains behind them to give us some privacy. I set my mug on the table, rise, and start digging through the clothing while she finishes her tea.

I select things I want to see her wear, as well as pieces she'll probably feel the most confident in, and bring them over to her on the couch. They are all lovely shades of jewel tones: garnet, black, silver, and forest green.

"They are beautiful," she says, shifting the hangers to look at each piece.

"Do you want to take a look and decide for yourself?"

She shakes her head, her eyes roving over the details on everything I've picked. "I feel like you chose exactly what I would have liked. Maybe you missed your calling as a fashion designer."

Instead of answering, I reach over the clothing and drag her up by the hips to stand between my knees. "Let me help you get undressed then, so you can try a few things on."

She lifts her hands away so I can open her jeans and work them down her legs. The second her panties enter my line of vision, my mouth waters to taste her, but I don't. Once I've stripped off everything except her underwear, she leans over and drags the clothing closer to try them on.

One by one, she moves through the clothing until she gets to the final few items, which are all dresses I know will cup her figure and show off all her assets. I almost hate to buy them since no one will see them but me if I have my way. Except that's not the point of this venture. We need her memorable and looking every inch the fucking queen she is.

"How are they?" I ask, leaning back, my knees splayed, with her still standing between them.

She skims her hands down her hips, smoothing the dress. "I feel…sexy. I like them. Are you sure about this? I can grab a couple of items, just enough to play the part, and save you all the money."

I sit up and cup her hips to pull her into my lap properly. She has to maneuver the dress almost all the way up to her waist to keep from ruining it, but I don't care. "Do you think I give a shit about money? I'd spend it all on you if it would make you smile."

Her answer is to lean in and give me a deep kiss, her tongue finding my own easily. I moan into her mouth and tug her hips tighter against me. Yes. This is what I need. I cup my hands around her ass and knead her cheeks to increase the friction between our bodies. When she breaks the kiss, I lean toward her, intent on chasing her mouth with my own, but she presses her fingers there instead.

Fine. I can work with that. Gently, I draw one of the digits between my lips and suck hard enough to send her rocking against me. Then I nibble her fingertip and move to another, again laving it with my tongue.

"Will you behave?" she whispers.

I let her pop her fingers from my mouth. "Why? No one will interrupt us because I told them not to come back until I say. Trust me, they want the tip they are going to get better than checking in on us every five minutes."

She pressed into my chest, mashing her breasts against me. "In that case..." Her mouth tips down again, taking mine slowly, teasing me with each renewed brush and heavy breath.

When we break apart again, I'm hard and rocking up against her panties. At this rate, I'll come in my pants from just the dry fucking. "Let's finish things up so I can take you home and make love to you properly."

Her lips glisten in the overhead light, begging me to drag them between my teeth, but I don't. Instead, I carefully ease her off my lap so she can get dressed while I stack our purchases and send a text message to Tricia.

We don't stay for the check out. I give Tricia the information she needs and drag Valentina to the car by the hand. Once we are inside, I settle her across my lap again, keeping her thighs spread wide over my own, enjoying how she arches her hips into me even though layers of clothing separate our naked skin.

"Soon, Angel," I say, cupping her face in my hands to control her mouth while I kiss her deeply.

She tastes like salvation, and lord knows I need the deliverance more than anything else.

"Is it always going to be like this?" she whispers against my lips.

While I don't have much experience with healthy relationships, I hope it is. So I shrug. "I don't know, Angel. But I can tell you that I'll never stop wanting you. Not while I have breath left in my body. Even if you curse me, hate me, fight me...I'll always want you. You're mine."

She swallows loud between us and drags my face closer to hers. "You're mine too."

27

VALENTINA

Only a few days are left until the society's deadline. I feel each one slipping through my fingers, my chances to defuse the situation and save all of us going along with it.

I've tried everything I could think of. Talking to Sal's family was the worst kind of torture, but I still did it in hopes that it might save him. Of course, they took pleasure in mocking me and no doubt will continue to do so until the day we all stand on even ground.

I poke at my breakfast, oatmeal today, and I don't mind. After most of the staff left in favor of safety, I was surprised when Adrian whipped around the kitchen as if he'd been cooking all his life. It occurred to me then, and still does today, how little I know about him. Especially his past. I know who his family is and how painful things have been for him, but I don't know his hobbies or what he likes to do when he has free time. Not that I've seen him have any such things since I've moved in with him.

It's always been about me or us, so I haven't been able to have any real downtime with him.

He eats his breakfast while he reads his emails, and I watch him, my heart in my throat. Every second closer to the summons is one less second I have with him.

I set my spoon on the table and clear my throat. Subtle.

He glances over his bowl at me. "You okay?"

"What if instead of answering the summons, we just run away instead?" It's a question I've been asking myself for days. We would both be safe, selfish to think of ourselves only, but I'd be able to keep him for longer, and our child would remain safe in the process.

With a swipe of his finger, he closes his phone and lets it clatter to the table. "Excuse me?"

I try to explain what I mean. "What if you don't answer, and we just run...we have enough money and resources. Both of us could disappear and start over with very little effort."

"This is...Why are we having this conversation? What got this idea in your head?"

I shrug and consider picking my spoon back up to get out from under the intensity of his gaze. "It's just something I've been thinking about. I don't want to lose you."

"Angel," he snaps. "Look at me."

When I drag my eyes to his, he gives me one slow, deliberate headshake. "Nothing is going to happen to me, first of all, second…tell me why both of us making a run for it hasn't been an option on the table so far?"

I lick my lips and rack my brain. "I don't know."

"No matter how far we tried to run, the council would send people after us, and the more they have to chase you, the worse your punishment is for defying them."

It's my turn to level him with a petulant glare. "So we just let them lord over us all like that? To tell us when we can come and go, all at their bidding? How is that fair?"

He scoffs, and it makes me want to throw a pastry at his face. "Fairness is a concept for children. Life is never fair, and the council is even less fair than that. They work for themselves and themselves alone. Maybe one day we can destabilize their power enough to try to challenge them, but that day isn't today."

I stare into my breakfast and refuse to let him see the tears pooling in my eyes. It's not his dressing down that is making me cry. Again, it's the thought of us running out of time and quickly. Too quickly.

A warm hand slides against the back of my neck, then down the back of my shirt to ease along my spine. "Angel," he whispers, then removes his hand and kneels beside my chair. "Things will be okay. You will be okay, I promise you that. And you know I don't make promises lightly."

"It's not even about me. It's about what they will do to you. Not only for defying them, but for Sal's death, and if they suspect you, my father's too," I say, more to my food than to him.

He cups my chin in his fingers and slowly turns my face to meet his eyes. "They wouldn't dare take me out right now. Not when the season isn't for another couple of months. When it opens again, we might have trouble. For now, they want to scare us and set me straight is all."

I open my mouth to say something, anything to convince him, but there's a resignation to his gaze that stops me. I have nothing left to use to persuade him. And there's no one else I can talk to who might interfere to stop the meeting in the first place. God, I hate to feel so powerless. Each second closer strips away more and more of the self-assurance I've built up since we married.

Maybe that's why I hate them so much. They make me feel like a victim all over again. I resent them for it.

He stands with a sigh and returns to his spot on the other side of the table to finish his breakfast. Despite his insistence, I keep going over scenarios in my head, of ways we might be able to escape, of people who might be convinced to help us. I'm not above paying someone less reputable to help, as long as they aren't as bad as Sal's family…or well, in the same business. I couldn't stomach the thought of giving human traffickers those kinds of resources.

"Angel, you're still thinking pretty hard over there," he says, almost conversationally, but there's an edge to his tone that belies the casualness.

"It happens on occasion," I snip back and shovel another bite of oatmeal in my mouth.

He stands again, marches around the table, draws me out of my chair by my upper arm, and drags me down the hallway. I stumble behind him, my spoon still in my hand. "Where are we going?"

"You used to ask a lot fewer questions," he says over his shoulder, then opens the door to his armory.

I follow him in because he doesn't give me a choice, and the smell of the guns sends a wave of nausea through me that might bring up my breakfast.

After he finds the table with the knives, he shoves a few out of the way, lifts me up, and sets me on the stainless-steel table. I squeak and settle against the chill on my bare legs below my skirt. "What are we doing in here?"

He lifts a knife by the blade and slaps the handle in my palm. I jump so hard I almost drop it, but he clamps his hand around mine at the last second. "Calm down. I'm going to show you a few things, so you feel safer and also see that I can handle myself... even if the five aren't with me."

I swallow hard and nod. "Okay...what do I need to know?"

He repositions my hand and then lifts my wrist to move up and down. "Hold it like this and always come from below, never above."

"Or I could just not stab anyone at all."

He waves behind him. "Do you want a gun instead? I can teach you that next."

The man has made his point. I stare down at the gleaming edge of the knife. "What do you want me to do with it until I might need to use it? If we get to that point, then I'm pretty screwed already, right?"

His hand tightens, and he locks his gaze to mine. "We made a deal...you protect our child with your life. If I'm down, and they are coming at you, you still try to protect yourself, understand?"

I nod and try to press the knife into his hand. "Can we put this away now? I don't need it here."

His eyes shift down to where I'm holding the blade, and I follow his gaze to watch our hands clutching it almost on my lap. "Not until I show you how to use it."

"Oh my God, you're so weird. I'm not going to stab you, even if you'll enjoy it."

The corner of his mouth ticks up the tiniest hint. "Funny, Angel."

He lifts our bound hands and presses the tip of the blade to his neck a couple of inches below his solid jawline. Then he grabs my free hand and uses it to press my index finger into the groove of his neck muscles there. "Here, feel how soft it is. This is a great place to stab, especially with a shorter knife, all damage, no bone impact unless you hit the spine."

He's clutching me tightly, so tightly I'm afraid the point is going to cut into his skin any moment. "Understand?"

I nod, a little scared of the demonstration while a little turned on by his knowledge and confident execution. This is a man who can keep me safe, and my cavewoman brain loves it.

His hand comes off mine, clutching the knife, and curves around my low back. "Now lean forward, Angel, bring your hips to mine."

He doesn't have to tell me twice. I scoot forward, the steel making uncomfortable noises under my bare thighs and now bare ass since my skirt has ridden up.

I hike my legs up around his and lock my knees there. He brings my arms up around his neck like we are about to slow dance in high school. But when my hand with the knife curls around his neck, he guides the point of it right between his neck and his shoulder blade on the outside of his suit jacket. "There is another soft spot. The knife will sink right in, then leave it and run. They will spend time spinning around, trying to dislodge it while they bleed out very quickly."

My throat feels tight with his sexy mouth so close to mine, talking about murdering a man, of all things. "Any other tricks you need to show me?"

"Mmm...not with the knife." His mouth takes mine in seconds, dragging my bottom lip between his teeth and nibbling until I moan loud enough for him to hear. Then he kisses me again and trails his hand up to take the blade out of my grasp before I do some real damage in my lust-fueled haze.

I think he's going to put the knife away now, but instead, he brings it to his throat and wraps my hand around it again. With a gasp, I break away from his lips and stare down at it. "No way, I could kill you."

He leans into the blade and draws a very faint red line across his skin. I blink against the contrast and skip my gaze up to his eyes. They are bright and heavy-lidded. It hits me that he's trusting me right now. Trusting me with this thing he considers a vulnerability.

I don't need to see anything else. While holding the knife in one hand, I open his pants and drop my hand inside to find him hard, pre-cum already leaking from his broad tip. If we were in bed, I'd take him in my mouth, but right now, I just want to help him take the edge off.

I work him fast and hard, watching his face and the knife at the same time for any more blood or any signs of pain. All I get is heavy panting, then he leans his forehead into mine as I work him harder, my arm holding the knife going tingly from the exertion.

"Harder, Angel, make it hurt."

I groan aloud at his orders and dig my nails in a bit as I pump him hard in my hand. When he comes, it's with a grunt and hot jets of cum that make my hands slick. The second he eases down enough and stops shaking against me, I drop the knife, letting it fall to the floor.

Now, all I need is him to ease my own razor-sharp need. And after that hot as fuck stunt, I want to cut him to shreds.

I reach for him, and with a bold stare and a line of blood on his collar, he drops to his knees and flips up my skirt.

His gaze promises pleasure, but it also promises pain. Between us, there are always both.

28

ADRIAN

The day of the summons arrives cold and clear. I couldn't sleep and spent most of the night watching Valentina as she slept fitfully. If I could take the haunting from her eyes, I would, in a heartbeat. If I could save her from this, I'd endure any trial.

Kai pacing in the hallway lets me know it's time. I hoped to slip out before she noticed, but she grabs my hand tightly in hers when I shift to the edge of the bed. "You weren't going to sneak out, were you?"

"Considered it," I admit.

Tears coat her eyes and then slip down her pale cheeks, curls sticking to the wet trails. "Come here," she whispers.

I crawl across the bed, shoes and all, to take her into my arms one last time.

When I told her the council wouldn't try to take me out, I lied, and I lied well. They want nothing more than to wipe me off the face of the earth so they can take over my little piece of it. So I can't challenge them as I have been since my father died.

She's so soft and warm in my arms I don't know if I can bring myself to let go. Her hands roam down my chest and latch onto my belt buckle.

"Angel…" But there's no real fire in it. Not until she leans out to capture my lips in a kiss that threatens to melt my bones.

Her fingers turn frantic to open the belt, and my cock turns to iron as she delves her hand inside my boxer briefs and cups me tightly.

"One more time," she says. "I need to feel you inside me right now. Please."

She's already working my pants down to my hips, and I trail my hand up her bare thigh to find her curls already soaked for me.

It takes seconds to roll her over, bring her ass to my cock, and slip inside her wet sheath. She sighs against my forearm, cradling her head as if she's been waiting to feel me for ages and not hours.

I clasp her hip and pull her to me while I surge forward. I'm already about to come between the frenzied need for her and the way her cunt clenches around me so sweetly.

When she whimpers, I trail my hand over her hip and delve my fingers in to find her clit. I skim it gently, and she trembles against me. "How does that feel, Angel?"

"Perfect." There's a tremor in her voice too, and I push away my own feelings to focus on her. I can give her this. One last time, I can make her feel good.

"Push back against me. I'm going to make you come so hard."

She follows my orders, and I trace the curve of her thigh back to her hip and then her tight little ass. It takes some maneuvering to squeeze my hand between us, but the second I swirl my thumb around her hole, she gasps.

I gently feed my thumb into the little ring of muscle, and her hand shifts down to take over at her clit. "Come for me, Angel. Let me see you fall apart."

She shivers again, and I watch her face as she squeezes her eyes closed and then shudders so hard her knees knock together.

"That's it." She's so perfect. So fucking perfect. I pull my hand away from her ass, grab her hips and slam into her body a couple more times. That's all it takes to follow her into my own orgasm.

After, I carefully ease away so I don't mess up my suit and clean us both up. When I return, tears ghost across her eyes again. "Change your mind."

I sigh and shake my head. "We already discussed this. I have to go."

"Change your mind," she repeats more firmly.

This time, I give her a kiss on the forehead, then the lips, and head toward the door where Kai is waiting for me.

He thinks he's going with me, but I order him to stay behind, guard Valentina, and don't let those bastards get to her no matter what. "Guard her with your life. Understand me?"

With a clenched jaw and red eyes, he nods once. Anger in every line of his body. He can stay pissed at me for all I care. At least he'll be alive.

The drive to the meeting location is short, and I'm surprisingly clear-headed with the scent of my wife on me as I enter the building. Two men stop me just inside the doorway and pat me down head to toe. "Someone worried?" I quip.

My face splits open in pain, and I blink a haze out of my eye and stare down at the edge of a semi-automatic weapon the guard used to clock me with. I meet his eyes and hope he sees his death there because if I get out of this, he's going down first.

The second guard grabs my upper arm and hauls me forward. I've got some height and weight on him, so I don't make it easy. They take me to a door, zip-tie my hands, and then trot me inside. Around a conference table sits the current heads of the council, and I stare down every single of those motherfuckers and hope to put the fear of God into them.

One of the guards kicks my knees out and then bashes me in the side of the head again for good measure. A trickle of blood leaks into my ear, but I can barely feel the pain. For me, this is foreplay. I give the council a smile and wait.

"Adrian Doubeck, you are here on charges of murder. You know killing outside the season is prohibited and punishable by death," the woman at the head of the table intones. Her voice is bored as she reads the rap sheet like it's a grocery list.

I stay silent. It was the first thing I learned from my very overpriced attorney. Say nothing, deny everything if compelled to speak.

"Do you have anything to say for yourself?" she continues, her eyes still on the tablet in front of her.

I keep quiet and take another hit to the head, this time a punch instead of the heavy metal of the guard's weapon. I guess they want to keep me conscious for some of this, at least.

Finally, the woman looks up and meets my eyes. There's nothing in hers. It's like staring into a frozen wasteland.

She purses her lips, creating fine lines around her mouth. "Nothing?"

"You guys are going to condemn me anyway. Why should I help you?"

Her hands come up to wave at the collective. "Maybe we won't. This is a trial, not an execution. You have nothing to say about the deaths of two high-profile society members who were your known enemies?"

I lick the blood off my lip and smile again. "Who were those again? Maybe you could remind me who I have supposedly killed?"

She sighs. "This is ridiculous. We aren't going to get anywhere with him unless we escalate things. Bring in the girl." The last was spoken to the guards, one of whom walks out of the room at her order.

My mind is racing. What girl could they be referring to? I lock eyes with the woman, her gray-streaked hair pulled severely back against her head. I can't remember her name to even threaten her properly. "If you—"

The door opens again, and I jerk around to stare while Valentina is shoved into the room, but it's not a guard behind her. It's Andrea.

I'm on my feet in seconds, but I don't make it to Andrea before the other guard knocks me down again, then uses another zip tie to secure me to an iron loop in the floor. "You fucking traitor," I spit at her, trying to get free to launch myself at her.

Valentina is shaking, her knees bruised, her curls mussed from a ponytail. There are tears in her eyes, but her chin is steady, and she shakes her head at me. "I'm okay. Calm down. Calm down."

I glare at Andrea while I speak. "I will cut you up piece by fucking piece and feed you to the river. Once the fish get you, I'll find those fuckers too and skewer each and every one of them."

Andrea cranks up her chin. "That's colorful, but this is for your own good. Trust me."

I'm vibrating with my rage, my heart beating so fast there are black dots in my vision.

"Mr. Doubeck," the bitch at the table snaps. "May I have your attention, please. As you can see, we are prepared to take measures to make you talk. Save us the time and energy and confess now."

I open my mouth, for once prepared to do exactly as she says, but she cuts in before I can speak. "Or maybe we should be trying your lovely wife at this tribunal? She is the one with the closest connection to both the missing Novak leader and the other one... her fiancé, was it?"

Her cold eyes cut to Valentina, who thank fuck tells them nothing and holds her chin high.

"Nothing," she adds. "Let's up the ante then..."

The door opens one more time, and Kai is dragged in behind another guard carrying another gratuitously sized gun. They throw him to the floor between Valentina and me. "Another suspect for us to consider," she deadpans, still completely disinterested.

Kai rolls to his side and coughs up blood. His face is beaten to high hell—worse than mine. I glance up at Andrea. "Your doing?"

She shrugs and presses her gun harder to Valentina's temple. "He was asking for it."

I move to launch myself at her again, but the zip tie won't budge, not even the tiniest bit to get my hands freed. "I'm going to slaughter you," I say carefully. "So slowly you will feel every slice until there is nothing left but your brain and your heart to cut out."

Again, she seems disinterested in my threats. I shift my eyes to Valentina. "Tell them nothing, no matter what happens to me."

She blinks at me and then looks toward the council again. Her eyes are rimmed with tears, but she keeps her lips clamped tight.

The woman sighs, and I scramble for her name because she is my first target when I get out of here, after Andrea.

Everything in my body aches, but alongside it, the betrayal is so much worse. How could she do this to us, help them when they hurt her so badly. I lock eyes with her again, ignoring the woman waiting for me to say something. "Why? Why would you do this?"

Andrea smiles, and it's slightly unhinged. "They gave me exactly what I wanted. Sal's brothers in exchange for Valentina and Kai. An easy trade…"

I shake my head. "We were going to get them together."

"No," she spits at me. "You were going to get them, and I guarantee what you had planned is nothing compared to what I'm going to do to them both. What you have planned for me right now is nothing compared to how they will end up when I get my hands on them."

I flap my uselessly bound hands toward the council. "These assholes aren't exactly reliable. Who says they don't take us, kill you, and be done with it all."

Another smile. "Don't worry, I have leverage."

Now I'm curious…did she capture another of the five? I can't believe any of them would go along with this insane plan of hers. To betray me. To betray all of us.

"Leverage?"

She shifts her gaze to the table. "Didn't you notice? You don't have a full tribunal today. One of their numbers is missing."

29

VALENTINA

Oh, this plan is such a bad idea. When Andrea and Kai walked into my bedroom, Adrian was already gone, so I didn't think to argue. Why would I when it gave me what I wanted? But...standing here, watching them hurt him, I can't take much more of it before I lose my shit completely.

The council, as usual, doesn't care about anyone but themselves. Hell, the only reason Andrea could get this to work was because she spotted a lone council member doing some dirty things on her spy mission. The blackmail after that, to get him to comply, was easy enough for her as well.

I'm shaking, and I can't stop the tears pouring down my cheeks. He's bruised and battered all over. It hits me like an out-of-control car on a freeway...he lied to me. The man stood in front of me and told me they wouldn't try to take him out. From what I can tell, they are just doing it slowly and painfully to draw out his misery. Next, they will use me, but I'm not going to allow it if I can help it.

I jerk my arm, pretending to try to cut loose from Andrea's hold. It shocked me how easy the indifferent betrayal act came to her and how real she made it seem with Kai hunched over beside us. To be fair, that had been the hardest part. Watching her and the council guards beat up on him to subdue him.

Now that we are here, however, I'm not seeing a way for us all to get back out. Andrea maybe, if she keeps playing the part of the betrayer…at least until word eventually got back to the rest of the five. Otherwise, why wouldn't they have us all killed right here, right now? They obviously have the ruthlessness for it.

The question is, if someone else confesses to these crimes, will it mean they let Adrian off the hook, or will they still just murder us all? It's hard to think with all the guns in the room and the head councilwoman's cold eyes boring into me. Despite my fear and the trembling I'm sure they all see, I push my shoulders back and raise my chin. Adrian would want me to be strong, act like I belong here, that these people are beneath me

In this one tiny act of defiance, the council settles, the chairwoman waving at me. "You, Novak girl, do you have something to confess? After all, it is your father who is missing and presumed dead. And it wasn't a secret how little he cared for you."

Ouch. That kind of stings. The fact that strangers knew so much about my abuse, all the things my father put me through, and did nothing makes me hate these people even more. "I don't know if I have something to say yet. Are you willing to listen, or are you just going to pass judgment as you see fit and kill everyone anyway?"

"Valentina," Adrian snaps. "Be quiet."

I throw him a glare just as a guard comes up behind him with a gag and threads it across his mouth to secure behind his head. Despite his inability to talk, he's saying everything he needs to with his eyes.

He's telling me to let him handle this. To let him die to protect our child and me. If he really knew me, he'd know how impossible it is for me to let him die this way. Not for me. But I'll keep my promise to him and ensure our baby lives, no matter what.

The councilwoman sneers at Adrian. Like the sight of a bound man turns her on. Yet another reason to hate her. There is definitely something in her eyes as she stares down my husband, bloody and broken before her.

This baby is my only leverage right now. If they know of its existence, then they might want me dead regardless. If I confess it and force them to make a deal with me, then I might be able to keep the little one safe.

"I do have a confession, Councilwoman, but only if you make a deal with me."

Her beady eyes narrow as she scans me from head to toe. "Let me guess, you want me to save your lover?"

I flick my hand toward Adrian. "Save him from what? His mouth? Once you hear my confession, you'll have no choice but to find him innocent and release him anyway. I know you guys follow your own rules here, but to kill him unjustly without provocation? Well, I think some of his supporters might have something to say about that."

"No matter, I can easily say you were both in on it. You both carried out these murders to usurp and take over society and this council."

I shrug. "Well, if you want to take the risk, that's your choice. But I'm offering you another way. A signed and sealed confession. All you have to do is make a deal."

Now, it seems, I have her full attention. The other council members murmur in each other's ears, and then they all fall silent and look at me.

Adrian squirms against his capture, trying to speak, raging against his restraint. I can't risk even glancing over at him for fear I'll lose my nerve. Not when there is so much on the line. My fingers are numb, my face is hot, and I'm about five seconds from passing out. Hopefully, Andrea will still catch me even if I keel over on her.

"What sort of deal do you have in mind?"

Andrea tightens her grip on my arm, but I don't glance at her either. "Not the kind I'm going to announce beforehand. I can promise it has nothing to do with letting anyone go free. That's the only hint I'll give you."

She scowls heavily, her nails clicking on the table. "Enough of these games. I'll just kill you all."

One of the other council members speaks up, an older man who I think I recognize as one of my father's old friends. "We should hear what she has to say. Many of us want justice for Novak. We want to give him a proper burial and see his killer brought in for punishment. If this girl knows or did the deed herself, I want to hear it."

It irks me the way he says "this girl" like he didn't practically watch me grow up and suffer so much abuse at my father's hand. Yet another example of the "mind your own business" boys club that did nothing to help me for years.

The councilwoman sighs heavily like she's really put out by all the talking she has to listen to today instead of all the bloodshed. "Fine, very well. We have a deal."

I shake my head. "In writing. Signed, of course."

Oh, by the look on her face, I'm pushing it now. She wants to rip me apart for daring to interrupt her proceedings like this.

Adrian lets out a loud noise to try to grab my attention, but I keep ignoring him, even as my body is vibrating with the need to touch him, to help him. The man who spoke before pulls a notepad from his jacket pocket and scribbles out a note, then hands it to the councilwoman.

She locks eyes with me as she slashes her name across the page. "This better be fucking good."

I take a deep breath and cup my belly low in the front. "You agreed, so thank you, that you won't kill me before my child is due."

The room goes silent. So quiet, yet so weighted with anger and hostility. Most of it seething off Adrian right now between Andrea and me ruining his plans, and now the council knowing our child exists.

"Very well," the councilwoman says, impatience crackling under every syllable. "Your confession then…"

"I killed them both. My father was a mean old bastard who did his best to make my life hell. Sal, who was my fiancé, brutally raped and murdered my cousin before he tried to murder me. So because of those things, I killed him too." I say this all deadpan like my insides aren't shaking apart piece by vital piece.

"You killed them. Two grown men? With no other help?" the older man asks. But it's not a question. It's all derision. He doesn't believe a word I've said.

I shrug, still trying to seem calm and at ease. "It's easy enough for a small woman to kill a man with a gun. My father tried to drug me and force an abortion, so I shot him in the gut and left him for dead."

The room goes quiet again, and for the first time in several minutes, I risk a glance at Adrian. Hoping he can see in my eyes that I'm doing this for him.

"And you," the councilwoman says, her attention also turning to Adrian. The guard steps away to remove his gag. He still can't stand, but he squares his shoulders and looks every inch the broken king, blood dripping off his chin like he's already taken a bite out of the world and plans to devour the rest.

I swallow against the wave of need and love that threatens to drag me down and make me take back everything I've said here.

"She is the last Novak, and she is carrying the heir to the Doubeck family line. She can't be killed, and you know it. I think the only person here who doesn't is her." He shoots me a look of contempt and pity that feels like a kick to the face.

The councilwoman scowls heavily at all of us and settles back in her chair. "It seems I have some considering to do. She confessed. The only people here who know she's the last Novak are in this room. I think killing you all and being done with this entire affair seems like the most prudent choice. Especially given the fact that you have a penchant for staying alive when people want you dead," she adds, her eyes grazing down Adrian's body.

I'm about five seconds from breaking Andrea's grasp, climbing over the table, and slamming this bitch's face into the mahogany if she keeps looking at my husband that way.

"Anything else to add?" She lets her eyes dip down to Adrian's thighs, where they stretch the seams of his suit pants in his restrained position. "Maybe we should talk privately, and we could come up with something."

"Don't you fucking dare," I whisper to him.

He cuts me a look. "That's rich coming from you. I told you I could take care of this, and you chose to disobey me and come here. You chose to endanger our child and ruin everything."

"Everything?" I counter, no longer trying to hide the hurt in my voice. "Your entire plan of getting captured and murdered? Because to me and Kai, that didn't seem like much of a plan."

"Kai is my employee. I don't pay him for his opinions on my behavior. You are my wife, and I didn't ask for yours either." He spits at the floor, blood spraying across the shiny concrete.

I grind my teeth and flick a look toward Kai, who is still slumped to his side, clutching his ribs. They must be broken. Andrea has a gun, but the guards have bigger ones. The small plan of creating a distraction and making a break for it won't work, not while we are all injured.

He's arguing with me, fighting me, yet I know somehow, it's an act. His words are there, yet I can tell he doesn't mean them by the set of his beautiful eyes.

So what's the game?

And how do we get out of here alive?

30

ADRIAN

I've never felt this mix of pride and hostility. Part of me hates her for defying my orders and coming here. The other part of me can't believe I managed to marry such an incredibly brave and selfless woman. Even after everything she's been through, she can still be my beacon in the darkness.

The councilwoman is waiting for me to counter my wife's offer, knowing she'd rather have my head on a pike than anything else. So I say the first thing that comes to mind. "Restrain my wife and gag her, and you and I can have a civilized conversation."

I hear Valentina's gasp from across the room but don't even glance her way for fear of losing the councilwoman's attention. There's no way in hell I'll sleep with her unless I could gain access to a weapon before she got me in her bed. But knowing what I know about our esteemed councilwoman, she'd have me tied to the headboard to take what she wants rather than be seduced.

She snaps her fingers, and a guard quickly produces a chair and ties her up, then uses the same gag they used on me to silence her. Andrea lingers at the corner of the room, and while I'd tried to attack her when they first arrived, I've had time to calm down and truly think things through. Nothing would entice Andrea into betraying me. She must be here on Kai's orders even though he doesn't look so great for the effort.

I can't think about any of them right now. This is my last chance to save even some of them, and if I can't save Valentina, then there is no reason left for me to live. I pin the councilwoman with a stare that used to make women shiver for me. In fear or anticipation, I've never known. Both if I have my way. It probably loses some of its effects with one of my eyes almost swollen shut and the bruising on my cheeks, but I do what I can anyway.

I know I've got her when she licks her lips and comes around the table toward me. One of the other men warns her about getting too close, and he's right. If I get her in the distance of my hands, she's a dead woman. But she stays far enough that I can't reach with my restraints holding me back.

"And what is your offer?" she asks, dipping her eyes down to my crotch and back up.

Valentina lets out something muffled like a curse, but now it's her turn to be ignored while I save her life. Unlike her, I know what I'm doing, and I won't fail.

I clear my throat and call on the indifferent mask I usually wear at society functions. "There are very few in society who know the inner workings like you or me. If I wanted to, I could hunt down every council member here, along with your families, your friends, your cats, your dogs, your household staff, and let's not forget your neighbors."

The councilwoman snorts. "This is your idea of a negotiation? Threatening us when you're tied to the floor on your knees."

I sort of shrug, but it's difficult with my hands bound to the floor. "You know what I'm capable of. You all do, as evidenced by the fact that I was able to take out a head society member's son, and then a family head himself...and you still haven't found him, have you? Don't worry, you won't. Not without my help."

She waves me on impatiently as she leans her thin hips against the table. "And...you're offering what? You just admitted your crimes. I can kill you now and defend myself against anyone in society who would like to argue about our rules."

"If you want...but you'd have to let everyone else go, and I guarantee my five won't let my death go unpunished."

She flicks her gaze to Kai, who is still groaning on the concrete. At this point, he's either seriously injured or playing up his injuries for a reason I haven't been able to figure out yet.

"So I kill you, and I get your bodyguards after me. I don't kill you and kill your wife and heir instead...then what?"

"It'll be both me and my five who come after you. Not the rest of the council. Just you. And I promise we'll make you pay for every minute they've been in this room. For every minute she suffers."

With another huff, then a chuckle, she stands and anchors her arms under her breasts as if she wants to emphasize them.

"What's in this for me? Your five come after me if I kill you, and then you come after me if I don't. Where does the negotiation come in?"

"Let Valentina live. Let her take over the Doubeck and the Novak holdings, and before you kill me, I'll ensure the five don't come anywhere near the council for it," I say.

It's a bold move to threaten them and then try to mitigate my own threat. It's only by the reputation of my men that she's considering it. Many in society fear them, as much as they want to steal them away for themselves.

I can see the gears turning in her little mind. It's worth it to her... she's going to ask for proof that I can keep them tethered even after my death. I don't bother sharing. I won't need to. The second I die, their duties will fall to protecting Valentina and my heir. Not a single one would fail to heed that dictate, or else Kai would ensure they learned their lesson the hard way.

As if he knows I'm thinking about him, Kai rolls over, his face swollen and bloody, and struggles to his knees. The guards immediately move in and secure his hands to another loop in the floor.

Excellent job decorating these assholes have done.

I turn my attention back to the councilwoman, who doesn't seem the least bit concerned by Kai's rousing. It's time to press her into a decision, and hopefully, one that doesn't have me playing horse to her rider. The very thought makes me want to gag. Death might be preferable.

"What do you say, Councilwoman? Do we have a deal? I'll want it in writing as well, as long as I'm being clear about things."

Her eyes narrow, and she stares back and forth between us. One by one, she looks, and she sneers, "I'm tired of these games. You're only stalling for time and making things worse for yourselves. From where I stand, I'll just kill you all and be done with the entire Doubeck and Novak lines. It will save me a lot of trouble and a lot of money once I bid on your holdings after your deaths."

I file that little nugget away to the back of my mind and scramble for something else to offer her. Something that will give me enough leverage to save Valentina and our child. Kai and Andrea brought themselves into this room, knowing my main priority would be my wife. Their fate is on them now. Luckily, I won't be alive to mourn my failures.

"Councilwo—" I begin.

She snaps her hand closed like a sock puppet. "I'm tired of listening to you speak. We are done negotiating."

A deep, ragged voice comes from behind me. "Then maybe you'll negotiate with me," Kai says.

I hang my head, cursing him. Why won't he stop when he knows he's lost? It's always been a flaw of his. No matter how hard he's hit the mat, he never stops fighting unless he's unconscious. I don't appreciate it right now, especially if it gets Valentina killed.

"Will you shut the hell up and sit there? That's an order."

Kai ignores me this time and directs his attention to the councilwoman. "You can put these individuals on trial if you want, but anything they confess is a moot point. I'm the only one in this room who knows where to find the bodies."

A liquid cold chill races through me, and I glance back at him again. "Are you fucking kidding me?"

Valentina struggles from her chair, her eyes filling with tears, locked on Kai. There's something they aren't telling me, something they planned, like this coup, that is about to get Kai utterly condemned.

"You forget, I can just kill you along with all your little friends."

Kai clears his throat heavily, coughing up blood. It dribbles over his lips and down his chin. "Well, considering I've been streaming this entire meeting to the society internet forums since I got here, I suggest you take my confession as a win and let Mr. and Mrs. Doubeck go free."

Her mouth pops open like a fish, and she stares at Kai for too long. When she gets her voice back, she stutters, "You l-lie. There's no way to get a signal into this building. You were searched for weapons; the guards would have found a camera."

Kai shifts forward and tilts his head down to one of the buttons on his shirt. "Not if they weren't looking at it the right way. I also happen to be good at getting signals in and out of places where they shouldn't. Test me, Councilwoman, or take my confession, lock me up, and give the Doubecks the courtesy they deserve as the reigning heads of two of society's great families. Or else... when it comes time to vote for council member seats again, you might have a little trouble getting nominated, no matter how many you take out of the running with your bullets."

Again, she flops her mouth open. The rest of the council is sitting up a little straighter, each casting their eyes around as if their invisible audience is in the room with us. Fucking Kai and his goddamn toys. I should have known he would plan something like this.

The sad part is, I can't even hate him right now. As much as I want to, this plan gets Valentina out of here. That's all I want. If I can get her to safety and keep her there, then I can come back for him later. With the five at my back, we are invincible. No one in society will stand up to us at our full strength.

"Kai," I whisper. "Are you sure about this?"

The guards are already releasing my zip ties and hauling Valentina out of her chair. Kai is stripped from the waist up and then resecured to the loop in the floor they used for me.

I jerk my arm from the guard's grip and stare down at my second in command, the man who always has my back. "Are you sure about this, Kai? If I can't get you back out of here before…"

"They won't execute me until they finish the trail. Thanks to my camera, every single one of these dicks will be on their best behavior from now on. You'll have a little time."

I nod and kneel, despite my bruises, and cup his face in my hands. He presses his bloody forehead to mine and nods. "If I don't make it out of here, though, you have to promise me one thing, Boss."

I nod, my throat too thick to speak now. "Anything."

"She's in the green safe house. She'll need to be moved since I don't know how much interrogation I'm in for. I can't risk her. I promised I'd keep her safe, and I have, but you need to go get her so she isn't taken by these assholes."

It takes everything in me not to glance to see if Valentina had been listening to what he said. Instead, I nod once and pat his swelling face gently. "I'll take care of it. Don't worry. I'll take Rose home, where she belongs."

31

KAI

It's quiet in the dark. Fuck, I haven't had this much silence in my life for years. It almost makes my ears ring. Every heartbeat seems to pulse in that noise until I take a long deep breath and let it out slowly. This isn't the first time I've been cornered, and it won't be the last.

My cell is concrete. The solid, thick kind that there's no getting out of unless released. So I wait. Adrian and Valentina won't let me rot in here. For all the things I've done, I trust them both with my life.

There's blood crusting my face, but I don't waste the very little water they've given me by washing it off. My knuckles are bruised from fighting the bastards, but there's not much I could do while being held down with someone's knee in my back as they batter me black and blue for answers.

My mouth twists into a smile. Answers there is no way in hell they'll be able to drag out of me. That's something they don't understand. I scrub at the dried blood, now itchy, with the heel of my hand. Pretty much the only part of my body not bruised.

When I took their place on the chopping block, they promised mercy, and I suppose not putting a bullet in my head immediately after my confession is their form of leniency. These people don't know the meaning of mercy.

And when I get out of this cell, I won't be the one to teach it to them.

It's been a week, by my estimation, hazy though it is. The only time I'm actually alert is during the short window in which they drag me out of the cell, hose me down, feed me a Viagra, and strap me to the councilwoman's bed. She's even more disgusting than I gave her credit for. Worse, she assumes everyone wants her. So even though I'm drugged and tied down, she thinks it's a seduction and not a rape.

When I get out of here, I'm going to make her pay for this and for what she orchestrated against Andrea. Her attack could only have been sanctioned by Henrietta, as she asked me to call her while she rode my dick without my fucking permission.

I close my eyes and squeeze them shut so at least I can tell myself the darkness is my choice. This is how I get through anything. Grab some part of it and make it mine. I'll get out of here and do the same.

Rose pops into my head, as she always does, and I feel myself calming, breathing deeper. It's a trick I learned when I first took her to my apartment outside the penthouse. If I stay calm, she stays calm. If she stays calm, things don't get broken, and I don't have to cradle a crying, screaming girl for way longer than I should.

Adrian warned me not to touch her, and I've mostly kept that promise. Any times I put my hands on her were for medical care or comfort. Nothing more. Even if I've thought about it.

There's a sound in the hall. That's the problem with concrete, it echoes loudly, and I've got excellent hearing. It's not the click of high heels, thank fuck, to alert me that she's asked for me again, nor is it the heavy drum base of the guard who's been pacing back and forth in front of my cell for the past two hours.

I think it's night. At least it feels that way by the chill in the air. I'm wearing nothing but the clean boxer briefs they gave me to wear this morning after Henrietta was through using me. Time is harder to discern. The guards change shifts every eight hours, and four are regularly on rotation outside my cell if their gait is anything to go by. I call one fatty with his heavy clomp clomp clomping step, one gimpy because he has a sort of drag to his step with every turn. One is skippy since he seems to run back and forth in the hallway, moving quickly, like he is trying to get a workout in during every guard shift. The last one is the meanest, and I just call him motherfucker. His steps are normal, at least for this lot, but his fists are rougher than the others, and he's not afraid to hit me.

My guess...Henrietta had been sleeping with him before she decided to get herself an upgrade.

I focus on the steps again, but there are several now. One I'd recognize anywhere. I've been listening to them pace the halls of the penthouse for years.

I tuck my legs up to hide my nudity and brace my arms across my knees so he can't see the bruises there.

The door is thrown open, but it's not Adrian who walks in, it's Valentina. Ah. She's light, tiny, I usually can't hear her walking around unless she's angry.

She takes a step into the cell with Adrian right on her ass. The guard closes the door behind them.

"Careful," I warn. "Now that they got you here, they might not let you out again."

Adrian digs his cell phone out of his pocket and flips on the flashlight so we can see each other. "This place is a shithole. Don't they know concrete isn't great for holding cells, too damn hard to heat."

I shiver as if proving his point, but it's more out of adrenaline from seeing them than the actual chill in the air. "What are you doing here? The stream I did should have given you guys time to get away."

He snorts and shoves the hand not holding his phone into his pocket. "You really think I'd leave you, just like that?"

I wave at his wife. "To protect Valentina and your child, of course, I would." Maybe he's fucking with me for defying his orders and coming after him even though he expressly forbade it. "And I sure as hell didn't think you'd be dumb enough to bring her back here, under any circumstance."

He meets my eyes head-on and shrugs. "It seems I can't deny her anything. Her only request every day for the past week has been to come here and get you out. Considering I also want you out of this hellhole, I was inclined to make it happen."

A bright light surges in my chest. "We're leaving?"

"Not yet," Valentina says, closing the distance between us. I stare at her, almost on equal height with me sitting on the bench and her short stature.

She strikes out, slapping me hard across the cheek. With the slap, she caught a little of my ear, too, setting it ringing.

I clutch my face and glare her way. "What the hell? Haven't I been beaten enough recently?"

"Watch your tone," Adrian hisses, stepping behind her to cup her upper arms and pull her back a few steps.

"Why didn't you tell me Rose was alive?" she demands, her fists clenched at her side.

I peer over her shoulder at Adrian and answer. "Why do you think? Orders. It's the reason I do anything that I do."

She waves around the room exaggeratedly, her arm casting shadows in Adrian's flashlight. "You seem to disobey orders just fine when it suits you, and I saved your life, or have you forgotten."

Guilt. Another old friend threatens to choke me, but I shove it down again. "I stand by my decision to keep her existence secret. It wasn't safe for either of you between Sal's family and your father. Besides, mentally, she still needs a lot of care. She has a hard time processing things, being touched, and even going outside. And there's one more major reason I didn't tell you."

Her hands frame her slim hips, her curls spinning around her face in her anger. "Yes?"

"She doesn't want to see you. We talked about it. She specifically told me she doesn't want to see you."

At my admission, Valentina gasps and steps backward into Adrian's chest. He immediately folds her into his arms, the light spinning to illuminate the floor. There's only so much he can protect her from, and the truth isn't one of those things.

I wait for her to get a hold of herself, praying it's sooner rather than later as I do want out of this shit box before Henrietta returns and they find out what she's been doing to me.

"Is that it?" she whispers. "Are there any other secrets I should know about? Any other lies you've gotten hidden up your sleeve waiting to ambush me?"

I shake my head. "No. I was tasked to take her to safety and keep her safe, and that's what I've done."

She freezes, her body going rigid. "Oh my God, she's been there all this time alone, and you haven't been able to check on her. What if she's hurt or ran out of food—"

"I put a system in place. She has a cleaning lady, Parker, who comes every week and delivers anything she might need in case I can't make it back to the apartment to check on her. Don't worry. I know how to keep a person hidden and cared for."

Something in her face says that is not reassuring in the least.

"I want to see her. I want to go get her and bring her home."

I meet Adrian's eyes over her shoulder. "Is that wise? She isn't wrapped up in this whole council business. As far as I can tell, the world has forgotten she even exists. Wouldn't it be better if we kept it that way rather than put her in the council's crosshairs too?"

Valentina looks as if she wants to argue, but after a moment, she drops her chin and shakes her head. "Maybe you're right. We should keep her safe, protected, until all of this blows over, and then we can bring her home like she deserves."

Adrian rubs her arms to comfort her.

A tiny part of me envies that comfort, the soft touch of human connection meant to heal, not harm. I seem to only ever get hurt.

She spins in his embrace and wraps her arms around his neck. I give them this moment even as I'm mentally rushing them to get me the hell out of here.

When Adrian releases her, she faces me again. "The live stream you did set some of our more avid supporters on edge. They are demanding a recall of the council, and you be put on a sort of bail until you can be retried for your—the crimes. We are taking you home with us."

I surge to my feet and keep my hands low so she doesn't see anything Adrian might kill me for later. Her eyes rove up to the ceiling once she realizes I'm only in my underwear. "They kept you like this?"

"It doesn't matter." I rush toward the door. "Let's go before they change their mind and lock us all in."

Adrian pounds on the cell door, and it swings open to reveal a guard. Fatty, I'd say, by the looks of him.

The guard steps out of the way, and Adrian invades his space. "Clothes. Now. I'm not taking him outside like this."

A voice cuts in from the end of the hall. "Oh, but he looks so nice this way. I decided to make it his uniform."

A cold chill cascades down my spine, and I squeeze my eyes shut. I'd hoped she wouldn't come, but why wouldn't she when she can rub her deeds in my face.

She steps closer and rubs her hand down my arm. "We had so much fun together, but it looks like you get to leave for a bit. Don't worry, I'll see you again soon."

I'm about one second from grabbing her and slamming her face into the wall when Valentina slaps her hand off me with a sneer. "Don't worry, I'll be seeing you again soon too."

∽

Thank You for reading Promise to Keep. Find Kai's story in Bound to Darkness.

ABOUT THE AUTHORS

J.L. Beck is a *USA Today* and international bestselling author who writes contemporary and dark romance. She is also one half of the author duo Beck & Hallman. Check out her Website to order Signed Paperbacks and special swag.

www.bleedingheartromance.com

Monica Corwin is a New York Times and USA Today Bestselling author. She is an outspoken writer attempting to make romance accessible to everyone, no matter their preferences. As a Northern Ohioian, Monica enjoys snow drifts, three seasons of weather, and a dislike of Michigan football. Monica owns more books about King Arthur than should be strictly necessary. Also typewriters...lots and lots of typewriters.

You can find her on Facebook, Instagram and Twitter or check out her website.

www.monicacorwin.com

Printed in Great Britain
by Amazon